THE LAST HIT

2/28/14

THE LAST HIT

LLWYD OWEN

For Tubbs; who inspired this novel.
If you're still alive, I hope you're well. If not, RIP.

First impression: 2013

© Llwyd Owen & Y Lolfa Cyf., 2013

Cover design: Jamie Hamley

The publisher acknowledges the support of the Welsh Books Council

ISBN: 978 0 95601 257 9

Printed on acid-free and partly recycled paper
and published and bound in Wales by
Y Lolfa Cyf., Talybont, Ceredigion SY24 5HE
e-mail ylolfa@ylolfa.com
website www.ylolfa.com
tel 01970 832 304
fax 832 782

"Outlaws only do wrong when they think it's right.
Criminals only feel right when they're doing wrong."

Jim Dodge

HIT NO. 47

I N THE heart of a dark forest, lit only by the full moon, lies a hole approximately five feet deep. Two figures stand next to it: one a permed, silhouetted, stereotype of a Scouser; the other a man-mountain from south Wales. One natters like an auctioneer on an assortment of amphetamines. The other stares in sombre silence as the scene unfolds.

"You don' avta do this, lar! You know, da follow t'ru, like. Come 'ead lar, don' be a meff. Waddyasay? Lerrus go, like. Wossit to you anyway, lar? I'll disappear. Blink and I'll be gone, lar. Into the night. Gone through the mist. Promise, like... on Stevie G's life, lar," blurted the skinny cunt with the curly hair.

"Shut up and keep digging," whispered the other – the one with the gun, wearing the black overalls – in a patient, but forced, monotone. He'd seen this tactic at work before of course. Too many times. That, unfortunately, was the nature of his profession.

He watched the stick-thin-scone-'ead digging his final resting place – his kinky afro shining in the moon's full beam, deep in the heart of this lonely woodland, somewhere in mid Wales.

"Come 'ead, lar," the Scouser started again. "I won' come back. I'll do one proper like. Serious now. I'm no divvy. No Joey. Do I look like a divvy? Like a Joey? Don' answer dat, lar. But I'll be gone, I guarantee you. For ever, lar. A-men an' all dat. Spain. India. Rio. Thailand..." But before Cilla's spawn has the chance to turn the forest into a geography lesson, the colossus slowly raised his gun level with *arrr Barry's* face, silencing his words with this stealthy action.

The scally dug deeper while the assassin kept eyes. With the mist hanging low above their private cemetery and the evergreen trees glistening under the special effects of the firmamental light show, the man with the gun wondered how many other bodies were buried in this part of Wales. Hundreds, if not thousands, was his conclusion… and he himself had contributed a fair few to that total.

An owl hooted nearby, reeling him back to the here and now. And as if the owl had cued him in, the tatty'ead started talking again.

"Come 'ead Tubbs, lerrus go, lar. It's no skin off yur nose, like…" and on hearing his ironic nickname, the Scouser had lost his very last hope of seeing another day. And although he didn't have *much* chance before uttering the word '*Tubbs*' he didn't have *any* now.

Tubbs cocked his gun. Then lifted it once again.

"Ok, ok! Don't be like that, lar. Don't be hasty. Take it easy…" pleaded the still-breathing-cadaver; a rotten smile on his face. But when he saw the lack of emotion staring back in his direction, he lifted his spade once more and got back to work. There was no escape. He knew that now.

In absolute silence, he dug his hole for another fifteen minutes; although a forest is never truly soundless, especially under a misty petticoat of darkness. Tubbs blew on his hands and regretted not bringing some gloves, and stamped from foot to foot to keep the blood circling around his huge body. At one point he even considered grabbing the spade from the Scouser's grasp and finishing the hole himself, but he binned that idea as it was no more than sentimentality. He'd always feel like this in the moments leading to the final act, and although he was very experienced at his job, that didn't stop him from being human. Every time, he would feel the shame tugging at him. And although he accepted that the man who stood before him deserved to die, he still didn't *really* want to be the one who would have to kill him.

He tried to clear his head. An impossible task. The sound of a nearby stream somehow soothed him, but the calm soon ceased when steel struck stone.

"Fuck me, lar! Me fuckin' wrist. It's on top te fuck. Might need to go to the ozzy, de'. Know mean?" With his wrist held tightly in his hand, the Scouser looked at Tubbs in the hope of seeing some compassion, or maybe even a little mercy. But he saw nothing of the kind.

Instead, he watched in silence as the Angel of Death lifted his gun once again, level with his sweaty forehead, before pulling the trigger without a second's hesitation.

In super-slo-mo, Tubbs watched as the scally's skull exploded in front of him, before his body fell limply into the open grave. Hole in one. But this course consisted of nothing but endless hazards – most of them slightly more serious than a bit of long grass, some sand or a lake. And no double brandies in the nineteenth either. Just regret, tinged with deep sadness and an overwhelming sense of enslavement. Due to the fact that killing someone, *anyone*, went against Tubbs's true nature, the sense of self-loathing was followed again tonight, as it always is, with a conflicting hatred for his mentor – the man who made him to live this way.

Regardless of the silencer, the loud crack appeared to have woken the entire forest and for a few seconds the trees were alive as the birds were startled from their slumber and the floor became a sea of small mammals rushing to find a safer place to snooze.

Tubbs stood completely still until the silence returned and the forest settled around him. Through glazed eyes he stared into the hole in front of him and noticed the Scouser's footwear. On his right foot he wore a relatively new, but very muddy, Nike trainer; while on his left he wore an orthopaedic version of the same shoe. He hadn't noticed his prey's disability earlier, but the realisation did nothing but add to the sense of guilt that was already feasting on his subconscious. Killing anyone is bad enough. But killing a reet is surely worse.

With nothing but shame coursing through his veins, one small mercy was that deciding which charity was to get half of his fee this time was an easy decision to reach.

With his gun still pointing at where the Scouser stood a few seconds previously, Tubbs focused on his weapon and remembered the first time he fired the beast. A single tear escaped from his left eye, rolled down his cheek and came to an abrupt stop on his stubbly jaw line. The hitman prayed to a god he didn't believe in that this would be the last time he'd be forced to fulfil a contract of this nature. But unfortunately for him he was bound to his mentor, so he shook his head to rid himself of that unattainable dream.

Tubbs grabbed the spade and felt the warmth of the Scouser's touch still clinging to the handle. But, like the stiff's soul, the heat soon disappeared into the surrounding darkness. He opened the large rucksack he carried with him on nights like these and emptied a bag of lye over the Scouser's still warm body. Next, he got to work and filled the hole in a fraction of the time his target took to open it, before concealing his handiwork with twigs and foliage collected nearby. After making sure that everything was well covered, he scattered the ground around the hole with a generous sprinkling of cayenne pepper to keep any nosy critters at bay, packed his bag, grabbed the spade, checked his compass and headed back towards his car, which was parked approximately three miles away in a dark lay-by off the A470.

Roughly halfway there, he dug another hole – this one only a few feet deep – before taking off his overalls and wiping the blood from his face with four baby wipes taken from his backpack. Into the hole went the garments, followed by a stream of petrol from a small canister, again taken from his rucksack. He lit a match and watched his clothes burn as he warmed his hands on the dancing flames. He squatted for five minutes, his eyes and ears trained on the surrounding darkness, before extinguishing the fire with earth and once again covering any trace with leaves and wood.

The lone wolf, clad in black from head to toe, trundled tiredly back to his car and the long drive that separated his home in the south from this latest ordeal.

He washed his boots and spades in a bubbling brook of the clearest water – and wondered if this indeed was the River Severn in its infancy; it was around here somewhere, he knew that for sure – before breaking the evergreen cover and stepping towards his car, which was tucked under a tall hedgerow in a murky lay-by a little north of Llanidloes. A cloud covered the moon as Tubbs walked. He felt more comfortable in the shadows than anywhere else, so welcomed its intrusion.

In the boot of the light grey VW Polo, Tubbs secured his gun and placed it in the secret compartment above the right wheel, before locking the bolt hole and making it disappear – as if by magic – and placing his bag and the spades on the tartan rug. While sliding his large frame into the driver's seat, he scowled at the pain caused by the fresh scars on his right leg. He bit down on the sleeve of his dark sweater until the soreness subsided. His latest tattoo – a fierce and fiery dragon – wound from the toes of his right foot around his foot, ankle and entire leg; all the way up to just above his hip. After three months of pain, it was almost done at last, but the worst part was yet to come and the next session promised nothing but torture as the details on and around the knee were to be filled in.

Cursing himself for forgetting the Preparation H, Tubbs looked at his watch – 23:17 – before starting the engine. The Polo started first time, as always, but the engine's near-silent purr made Tubbs nostalgic for his chopper, although there were a million good reasons for not using it as he went about his business.

Tubbs drove south for a few miles, without once exceeding the speed limit, before reaching the empty Llanidloes bypass where his heart began to flutter as he looked in the rear-view mirror. Keeping one eye on the road in front and the other on the car behind, the adrenalin surged through his veins, although in truth Tubbs knew he had very little to worry about. Even if it was the police, he was pretty certain they wouldn't find his gun even if they did pull him over and search the car. However, seeing that he wasn't driving like a twat and that the car's components – brake lights, for example, or any other fault that would draw their attention – were all working as they should, the cunts had no reason for stopping him in the first place. The light grey VW Polo was his secret weapon – a totally insignificant car, painted in the dullest and most inoffensive colour. Except for beige, perhaps. And of course, the 'borrowed', but clean, registration plates soothed his nerves even further.

Tubbs never used to be this confident though. In the past, during his 'wild days', being stopped was part of everyday life. Almost. But, considering he was delivering dope to customers across the length and breadth of Wales while riding a growling, souped-up, three-wheeled Harley complete with a Chinese dragon motif custom paint-job, a Bandidos flag waving in the wind and a trailer full of product dragging behind, that wasn't all *that* surprising in truth. Some seven years ago, Tubbs retired his chopper, and although he still rode it at least once a month, he never did when on a job. The light grey Polo was his trusty steed these days, and the fact that it was discreet, inconspicuous and unassuming was its strength… and right on cue, the car turned off the A470 towards Llanidloes itself, allowing Tubbs to breathe easy once again.

With the clock on the dash flashing half-past one and Merthyr

Tydfil sleeping uncomfortably to the left of the dual carriageway, Tubbs decided to go and see T-Bone, his boss now, instead of waiting until tomorrow. His earlier lethargy had lifted, and T-Bone rarely left the club before dawn anyhow.

T-Bone was Tubbs's employer in this particular field. But the head of the Bandidos branch of the Outlaw biker gang was much more than that in reality. After escaping from his biological father, T-Bone took in Tubbs and Foxy, his mother, before becoming his real dad in all but genes. And after his mother's murder, Tubbs and T-Bone grew ever closer. T-Bone was the *only* one who knew about this side of his life, and due to that fact, the old bastard had complete control over the young man's life. Tubbs didn't want to kill anyone, but he didn't want to let T-Bone down either. He owed him everything, after all. There was only one way to step off the path laid down for him all those years ago, and the master and apprentice had a verbal contract in place that would allow Tubbs to walk away from the killing floor if he ever found the man who murdered his mother.

FREEDOM TRAIN

W ITH '*I Feel Love*', the latest disco anthem to reach the top of the charts, spinning quietly on the stereo in the corner of her bedroom on the third floor of Dylan Towers on the Simcox Estate in Swansea, Foxy Mulldare was preparing to go to work.

On the bed, quietly watching his mother cover the latest in a long line of bruises administered to her face by his father, her pimp, lay Little Al. Little Al was *always* quiet. A six-year-old who'd never spoken a word. In fact, he'd never even made much noise during his entire life. He never cried. Never screamed. Never complained. Not even when he was a baby. This, of course, was a major cause for concern to his mother, and she blamed herself for bringing him into such a life. Was it any wonder that he was mute, when you consider the kind of man he and his mam were forced to live with?

As the foundation masked her yellowing shiner, Calvin Sweetman's voice could be heard disagreeing loudly with some local scum in the kitchen, where Al's father held his weekly poker game. The words of the busiest and most merciless pimp in Swansea sent a shiver up Foxy's spine. He was high, of that there was no doubt. He always was. Would an open palm be awaiting her later on? Or even worse: a closed fist? Maybe even a boot. There were so many options open to him.

"Right, time for bed, luv. Have you brushed your teeth?" Foxy asked, as she got to her feet and checked herself in the full-length mirror. Although her adult life had been very shitty in this pretty city, the years had been kind to her in terms of her appearance. And in her short leather skirt, knee-length PVC boots and leopard print boob-tube, she looked exactly as you'd expect a prostitute to look. Many of the other girls followed the latest fashion trends – which right now meant shiny, glittery, sparkly disco gear – and Foxy used to do the same at one time. One night last year, she wore a silver catsuit to work which made her look like a glitter ball on legs. But the costume proved to be very problematic, as a woman administering cheap thrills down back alleys – or if she's lucky, in the back of a car – needs easy access to her nether regions; something the cat suit couldn't provide. After that night, Foxy came to the conclusion that a prostitute should dress like a prostitute, so back she went to the mini-skirt and boots, in order not to confuse her customers, but also to minimise the time she had to spend in their company.

As she listened to Little Al brush his teeth in the bathroom next door, the guilt and shame she felt was almost overwhelming. Things should be *so* different. Life should be *so* much better than this. And as she listened to her tormentor's voice threatening some faceless thug in the kitchen, and the noise her boots made as she walked to Al's room to tuck him in, she felt so worthless, so ashamed and disappointed. Mainly in herself... no, *totally* in herself. She was the *only* one responsible for the situation she now found herself in, and there was no one who could help her escape.

By the time Foxy reached Al's room – the only room in the house that felt and looked almost normal, with its childish posters, scattered toys and bookshelves bursting with colour and unattainable dreams – the youngster was already in his bed, his dark eyes staring at her above the tatty and torn Superman duvet, pulled tightly to his chin. Foxy would have loved to get him a new one, but Calvin looked after the money.

The PVC squeaked as she crouched down by the side of her son's bed. In silence and with a smile on her lips, she stroked his dark curly hair while staring into his beautiful eyes. In them, she saw all her fears reflected back at her. Her heart broke once again.

"You ready to dream then, lovely?" She asked.

Al shook his head and produced a book from under the covers.

"I'll leave the lamp on for you then," added Foxy. "And remember to lock the door after I leave…"

Calvin had never touched Al – Foxy gave him that at least. After all she was his punchbag of choice, but she still insisted he locked the door every night when she left for work, as the simple truth was that she didn't trust the bastard in any way.

Al suddenly sat up and hugged his mam tightly. She almost started crying as Al never usually showed any kind of emotion – towards her or anyone else. He found communicating on an emotional level almost as difficult as doing so verbally. For some reason, this unexpected contact filled her with hope. Hope for what, she wasn't sure, but hope for something. Eventually they disentangled – although Foxy would have gladly stayed there all night – and as she stood, her boots squeaked again, which made Al smile.

"Love you," whispered Foxy, as she blew a kiss in her son's direction, before leaving the relative sanctuary of his room and stepping towards the lion's den that awaited her.

She wore her long leather coat and tied the belt around her waist, which made her tits bulge above the leopard print boob tube, like the Charlton brothers challenging to head the same ball, and breathed deeply to calm her nerves before heading for the door to the outside world, located on the far side of the kitchen, beyond the drunks playing their poker game. Calvin's voice was louder than any of the others – slurring and arguing, threatening and swearing. She recognised one of the others too – Jack the Bastard, a name that needed no explanation. There were another two voices as well, but she didn't know either of them.

With her head held high, Foxy aimed for the back door in the hope that no one would take any notice of her. As she strode, she saw the guns on the table – four of them – and felt the menace hanging in the air. Calvin – or 'Dirty Harry', as he christened himself after buying the Magnum that lay before him – owned the flat that was home to Foxy and Al, as well as the other three in this old Victorian terrace. It was a huge hostel for whores on four floors, with a girl in each bedroom. He lived in this one, with Foxy and Al, but regularly policed the rest and ruled his rotten empire with a tyrant's glee. He collected and kept *all* the money. Every penny. He imprisoned the girls with a cocktail of pharmaceuticals. Amphetamines usually, but also heroin in recent months. Thanks to Al, Foxy managed to avoid the hard drugs as Calvin didn't need to use anything else to ensure that she'd return home each night.

With the door within reach and the gamblers seemingly unaware of her presence, an open-hand smacked her hard on the backside, followed by a loud cackle from the fucked-up foursome. Her left cheek throbbed but the lack of respect hurt a whole lot more. It wasn't even Calvin who hit her.

After a quiet night down Swansea docks – if you can call three fucks, two blowjobs and a couple of quick hand shandies a 'quiet night' – Foxy returned home around midnight and slowly, in bare feet, climbed the stairs towards the flat. She always took off her stilettos on her return as she didn't want to draw any unwanted attention; and the last thing she wanted tonight was any attention from Calvin.

As she crept on tiptoes through the dark kitchen and lounge towards the relative safety of her bedroom, Foxy noticed that Calvin wasn't making a sound as he lay on the comfy chair in front of the television. She glanced in his direction and saw the empty bottle of Teacher's lying in his lap. The bottle would join the rest of the debris on the floor before dawn, when Calvin would stumble to his room. She took another step towards her sanctuary, then stopped and slowly turned her head once again. As the television's shadows danced on the wall and ceiling, Foxy could see that something wasn't quite right. She crept towards him, barely breathing; yet she could feel her heart pounding the inside of her ribcage, as if it too was desperate to escape.

She could smell the whisky as she drew nearer, as well as some unfamiliar metallic scent. Then she noticed the dark spots which speckled the wall behind the comfy chair. And finally the hole in Calvin's forehead. She tried to scream, but couldn't. No words spilled from her mouth. Only vomit. And as the bile cascaded, a million thoughts rushed through her head at once, all leading to the same place. The same person.

She turned and sprinted to Al's bedroom as the poker players' faces flashed in front of her eyes. The door was locked, so she grabbed her keys and struggled to find the hole. But there he was, her little angel, tucked up and fast asleep. She smiled, before the joy disappeared as she thought how sad it was that one so young could sleep through such a nightmare.

Then she thought of escaping. Of freedom.

She turned and left Little Al where he was and went to collect her money from Calvin Sweetman's private bank – a suitcase under his bed. Using a screwdriver she found in the kitchen drawer she managed to break the lock without too much effort. Unfortunately, the suitcase and its contents were too heavy to take as it was. She needed to hurry.

She filled a rucksack with cash – at least five grand if she had to guess – then changed her clothes. She threw her work clothes in a pile in the corner of her bedroom and squeezed her shapely twenty-six-year-old legs into a tight pair of denim jeans with sixteen-inch flares at the bottom. She slipped her feet into her favourite flat-soled boots – ankle, not knee length – and grabbed a sweater to cover her boobs. Then, with her heart almost breaking out of her ribcage, she filled a holdall with enough clothes to keep her and Al comfy for a few days at least, and returned to her son's bedroom to wake him from his dreams.

She sat on his bed. His eyes still closed, Al turned on his side, which moved the duvet and revealed Calvin's .44 Magnum lying by his side. Foxy shook her son in order to wake him, and in the room's low light, Al saw his mother's smile. A smile that turned to tears when her son spoke his very first words.

"Sorry, Mam," he whispered.

"Don't apologise, luv. Come on, we've got to go."

Foxy grabbed the gun and placed it in her bag, before helping Al to get dressed. Apart from the two bags, the only other thing she took with them that night was a few of Al's favourite books and a little palm in a pot – her birthday present from Al the previous year. She had no idea how or from where her son had got it, but apart from Al himself, that was the only thing she cared for in the whole world.

Hand in hand, they walked past Calvin without looking in his direction, through the kitchen, before Foxy opened the door a little and looked down the corridor for any sign of life.

"We'll have to move quick alright, luv. Ready?"

"Yes," answered Al – a trivial word if ever there was one, but a word that almost made Foxy weep.

RED EYE MORNING

THROUGH BLOODSHOT eyes and the thick cloud of cigarette smoke that clung to his head like a helmet, Gimp watched Vexl crush the pills into coarse grains on the kitchen table. In silence, the little man sucked hard on the Marlboro red, his eyes tracking his boss's hand as it went about its dirty business.

"I need some sleep, Vex," Gimp whispered, his voice so high pitched you'd swear his fags were filled with helium.

"Nah mon, yah nyeed summe nose-up on yah Cyornflakes, mon…" answered Vexl in an accent that dipped its toes in the Caribbean, a million miles from his roots in the Midlands of England, somewhere just north of Dudley. His pasty skin was blotchy. His teeth, yellow and black.

"Like Frosties, is it?"

"Yah mon," answered Vexl with a rotten grin, before plunging his head towards the table and snorting a huge line up his left nostril. Gimp watched as he flung his head back violently as if an unseen fist had just uppercut him unexpectedly. His whole body shuddered for a few seconds before he returned to his default position – fucked up.

Vexl hadn't slept for three nights, and claiming that he was 'close to the edge' was like saying that John Leslie likes his sex. Vexl felt like the end was already here. But what else could someone addicted to amphetamine-based slimming pills expect? The mashed up mayhem that lay in front of him on the kitchen table was the same drug he used to oppress his stable, control his workforce. Slimming pills from the sub-continent – a cheap, yet effective option. Highly illegal, of course, but perfect for this specific purpose. How the fuck did he get hooked? Vexl couldn't remember.

As the initial rush calmed a little, he sat back in his chair and felt for his trusty blade, which lay in its leather sheath under his right armpit.

Gimp trembled as he watched his boss go through the motions, but when Vexl handed him the rolled-up twenty, he took it and tightened it between his thumb and forefinger before hoovering the other line. The crystals burned like a bastard, sending a ball of flames deep into his body. He sat there for some time, riding the wave. Trying his best not to topple. To drown. How long this lasted, he didn't know, but when his eyes could focus once again, he saw the time flashing on the oven's digital clock. 07:17.

For a minute or two the pair sat in semi-silence, snorting and sniffing; ensuring that every crystal found its way into their bloodstreams.

With the morning light flooding the room, Gimp put on his shades to combat the strain. The silence was broken by the sound of footsteps upstairs. In response to the pitter-patter, Vexl reached for his knife and placed it carefully and quietly on the table between them, where Gimp was now dabbing the left-over crystals with his wet thumb.

Vexl looked at Gimp. Shook his head. Gimp gave him the bird, lit a fag. "Yuh sure yuh lyocked de door, mon?" whispered Vexl, his blood shot eyes flashing at Gimp through the dark vines that hung from his head.

"Course I fackin' did. Vat's an integral, if not ve most important part of ve scam, innit," whispered Gimp, as the footsteps descended slowly down the stairs.

The plan they were about to put into action was a simple one. It had to be. Vexl smiled, although it actually looked more like a grimace, while Gimp nodded as the pair listened to the early riser attempt to open the front door.

"Shit," came the cuss, before he started creeping towards the back of the house.

The man opened the kitchen door and froze when he saw the pimp and the gimp sitting at the kitchen table.

"Good morning, sir," said Gimp in his best butler voice.

"G-g-g-good m-m-m-morning," stuttered the man, as he rubbed his head with his hand.

"Wudjah like a cuppatee, mon?" asked Vexl, his accent tipping its toes in Trenchtown, masking the sarcasm and confusing the man that stood in front of him.

"Yes… I mean *no*… thanks… I've got to go… work… wife…"

"Then yah gotsta pay, mon," added Vexl, as he fingered the knife that gleamed in the sun's rays on the kitchen table.

"But I paid up front. Eighty pounds."

"Fah one hour…"

"B-but…"

"But naffin' my bruvva," added Gimp, as a calculator appeared in his right hand.

"Eighty notes an hour, right, and you've been ere 'ow long, mate?"

"Eight," Vexl answered on his behalf.

"Eight hours. That'll be six hundred and forty nicker then. Ok?"

The man shook his head for a few seconds but realised almost at once that disagreeing was totally futile, not to mention very foolish. He was a pretty experienced punter, and knew that this time he'd been well and truly stitched up. He'd never leave the house without paying, so he accepted his fate and reached for his wallet and credit card.

"No cards, mon."

"Cheque?"

"No! No fackin' cheques!" shouted Gimp before adding politely: "What d'you fink vis is, fackin' Tesco's?"

"Then I'm afraid I can't pay you…" said the man as he returned the card to his pocket.

"Don't be foolish, mon…" Vexl shook his head.

"You have heard of cash machines?" Gimp asked, as they both got to their feet and led the man out of the front door towards the car.

With the bright morning sunshine shimmering over the ocean, Barry Island had never looked better. But the town soon reverted to its true state – a total shithole – when a cloud covered the sun. Vexl lounged in the back staring at the man who sat beside him, while Gimp toked hard behind the wheel, propped up on a booster seat like some mutant monster child. The customer watched as the town rushed past the open window. He didn't feel angry or scared or anything, just a little daft.

LOOK INTO MY EYES

TUBBS'S EYES burned as he turned off the motorway and headed towards Caerphilly and the last stop on his journey home from mid Wales.

Following the slow drive through the heart of cheesetown, where he saw the usual dregs of society walking home from wherever, Tubbs found himself in the green belt between Caerphilly and Cardiff – where the countryside made its feeble attempt to keep the urban sprawl at bay.

He turned right opposite the Maen Llwyd pub in the heart of Rudry, and headed towards Lisvane before taking a right and driving carefully along an unsigned, unmarked and unkempt track, through a thick covering of trees into the heart of darkness.

Although Tubbs couldn't actually see his childhood home through the undergrowth, he knew it was there and, as usual, memories of his mother came back to haunt him, opening old wounds, and pouring salt on scars that could never heal.

This land, where Tubbs was raised by his mother and his mentor, belonged to T-Bone. The place that was so hard to return to since Foxy was killed. It still amazed him that T-Bone could continue to live here, but grieving affected everyone differently.

Tubbs remembered the time when T-Bone moved his headquarters here, back in 1987. Before then, the Bandidos' HQ was located on old industrial waste ground down Tremorfa, but after Tesco bought the land to build a huge supermarket to feed the residents of the myriad red-bricked houses popping up nearby, T-Bone was forced to find his crew a new home, and as it happened he already owned the perfect place.

T-Bone was a very wealthy man. He was rich when Tubbs first met him, which meant that he was far richer today. He chose his ventures carefully – drugs, arms, private security, the whole range. From plain shady to highly illegal; it didn't matter, as long as it made him money. The old man was still in charge and still open to new opportunities, which always somehow managed to turn a profit. He lived on his own in the eight-bedroom manor house, but spent most of his time at the office in the Bandidos' clubhouse, hidden from view on the other side of the sixty-acre estate.

Slowly, Tubbs drove along the winding track, which was like a portal to another world – a parallel reality that 'normal' people never witnessed, never experienced. As his eyes battled to stay open, he could hear his mother's voice calling to him from the trees, as their branches closed around him. He shook his head and rubbed his eyes, before slowing and stopping by the gateway to the club.

By the automatic gate stood two familiar faces – Chewbacca and Skid Row – wearing their dark leather uniforms, sporting hair like Terry Nutkins (which was the unfortunate reality for many a middle-aged biker), carrying a Kalashnikov each over their shoulders and passing a spliff as thick as a baby's bicep back and forth between them. They'd look pretty threatening to most people, but the boss's 'son' didn't have to worry about such matters.

Tubbs opened his window, before exchanging a little bullshit with them just to be polite. Not that he felt like it, but it was the least he could do. After all, he'd known these two lieutenants pretty much his entire life.

Beyond the gate, about a hundred yards further along the lane, the dark track reached the club's car park, which was pretty full tonight, as it always seemed to be; the chrome of the bikes glistening under the full moon's glare.

At the far end of the car park the clubhouse was teeming – bodies everywhere, music pumping and more testosterone than you'd find at a trannies' tea party. The building, which was tucked into and under a small cliff-face, had huge concertina doors at the front, which meant that the party couldn't stop itself from spilling out into the night, even when the place was relatively quiet. T-Bone's office was at the back of the club, so Tubbs would have to ruck his way through the throng to see him, which was the last thing he wanted to do tonight, because it was inevitable that he'd see someone who he knew.

He parked his car and heard a couple of voices chatting loudly as they left the club. Although the discussion came to an abrupt end as the pissed-up pair clocked the Polo.

"Ch-ch-ch-check this out!" One of them pointed, and stuttered and slurred his words after a long night on the Newkie Brown. "What the *fuck* is this *shit*? A *fuckin'* Veee Dubla… I'm gonna get my fuckin' crowbar…"

"Shuddup and get on yer fuckin' bike," the other countered as he saw Tubbs open his car door, wincing as the pain from the tattoo ripped open his leg once more.

"Fuck off, Sparks, anyone who drives a *f-f-f-fuckin'* Polo deserves a *f-f-f-f-fuckin'* pastin'…"

"Shut up, ya twat, before you get us both fucked up!"

"What?" asked Monkeyman, as his brain slowly caught up. His partner's tone of voice made him worry more than a little, and then he saw why, as Tubbs stood up and gleamed like a Greek god in the moonlight. He turned his head. Nodded.

"A-a-a-alright, Tubbs…" Sparkplug grovelled, pushing his partner along.

"Tubbs…" muttered Monkeyman.

Tubbs nodded and walked on. There was no point wasting any breath on these boys.

He stepped into the club and sidestepped his way through

the swarm. As usual, he was unarmed – as he always was when visiting the club – while every other Bandido seemed to be packing. He'd never carry his gun without reason, only when he intended to use it. The gun had some unexplainable hold over him, a power that Tubbs didn't like to contemplate too often. Certainly, the gun meant a lot to him. But it also knew too much…

The inside of the clubhouse was some kind of half-bar-half-garage type set-up, with all sorts of biker-related paraphernalia hanging on the walls. Behind the bar, in large letters, the Bandidos' motto read 'We are the people our parents warned us about', and next to it the gang's logo – a sombrero-clad gunman carrying a sabre – served as a centrepiece; while their scarlet and gold colours could be see all around, from the doors of the toilets to the patches on the jackets of most of those present.

Tubbs's intention was to see T-Bone, grab his cash and get out of there as soon as poss. He nodded to a few familiar faces playing pool – hairy men, one and all; wearing denims or leather; their bodies reeking of oil, sweat and booze; their skin covered in ink. The air was thick with the sweet smell of skunkweed, and the whole place made Tubbs feel very sentimental.

Tubbs almost made it through the crowd without wasting one second of his time, but as he limped tiredly past the bar, the unavoidable happened and he heard a familiar voice calling his name.

He turned and saw his best friend sat, shitfaced on a stool.

"Alright Bo', been here long?" asked Tubbs sarcastically. Not that Boda noticed.

"What you havin', then?" asked Boda, turning away from Tubbs and trying to get the attention of one of the barmaids. One of Boda's favourite parts of being a Bandido and having access to this clubhouse was the fact that the barmaids were all bollock naked. Tubbs on the other hand hated this tradition, mainly because his mam did this exact job for many years when he was growing up. And although no one forced the girls to strip, knowing that half the bastards in here had probably spanked one out over a mental image of his mother made him sick.

"Nothing for me, ta'. I'm here to see T-Bone. I'm knacked and need some sleep…" Boda's face couldn't hide his disappointment, but he didn't make a scene.

"Hairy muff, mon amigo. Late night delivery, is it?" He asked casually, stroking the ginger beard that hung from his chin. Instead of long hair like most other bikers, Boda shaved his scalp while his plaited beard tickled his torso.

"Something like that," answered Tubbs. He hated lying to his only friend, but he was an old hand at it now and had been doing so on two counts for far too long. And the other secret he kept from him was much worse as well. But he had no choice in the matter. T-Bone was the only one who knew where he'd been tonight, and that was the way Tubbs liked it.

"How's your leg?" asked Boda, slurping his double Jameson's.

"All right," lied Tubbs.

"Really? Why are you limping then?"

"I'm not limping!" smiled Tubbs, as he shuffled away from his friend. "I'll see you tomorrow for more pain."

"I'll be there around mid-day," promised Boda, before turning his back to get a better look at the view behind the bar.

Tubbs stepped to the door to the right of the bar – the one with 'Private – Staff Only' printed on it. After punching in the four-digit code on the lock, he opened the door and stepped out of the bar's smoky and noisy atmosphere into the club's quiet and peaceful business area. Tubbs hobbled towards the door to T-Bone's office and knocked lightly. He waited for an answer before entering – something he never used to do until he walked in on the old man boning one of the barmaids on his desk a few years ago.

"In," said a sleepy voice from the other side. The first thing that hit him upon entering was the almost overwhelming smell of Olbas oil. The place reeked like a Lockets factory but Tubbs didn't say anything. T-Bone slowly got to his feet. They shook hands. Hugged. He hadn't seen Tubbs for at least a week, maybe ten days. T-Bone stepped back to take a good look at him. Tubbs's size never ceased to amaze him, although there hadn't been anything 'tubby' about Little Al for many years.

Like a vegetarian called 'Beefy', Tubbs was an ironic nickname by now, although it was quite apt when he was first christened. After Foxy's death, T-Bone turned to the whisky while Tubbs took comfort in food. The young man ballooned in the months after losing his mother and was named Tubbs by some funny fucker down the club – a moniker that stuck forever. Al hated his nickname and made every effort to turn the fat into muscle, but it was too late even then and he'd been called Tubbs throughout his adult life.

"How are you, son? You look shattered."

"I am."

T-Bone offered him a seat before continuing with the conversation, although he didn't expect to hear much detail from Tubbs tonight. Al was always quiet, that was his default setting, but was always worse after completing a contract. T-Bone looked at him across his desk and felt the same emotions that he always did – grief and guilt.

"I'm not stopping..." Tubbs said, when he saw T-Bone reaching for the bottle of Laphroaig and two glasses. "I've got to get to bed. Another..."

"Busy day tomorrow," T-Bone finished his sentence and smiled. "That's a shame, I feel like I haven't seen you for ages. Not *properly* anyway..."

Tubbs shrugged, so T-Bone got up and headed for the safe in the far corner.

Tubbs watched his sixty-eight-year-old frame shuffling across the large office, and remembered the T-Bone of old, the muscle man on his shining Harley who gave Foxy and Little Al shelter when they needed it most. The scars could still be seen on his body – the stump of a left ear, the burn marks on his neck – following his near fatal crash just over a decade ago. It happened a few days after Foxy's murder. T-Bone disappeared on the back of his bike before being found later the same day in a roadside ditch not far from Libanus on the Brecon Beacons – his body as wrecked as his broken heart. Tubbs heard the rumours about the suicide ride, but never asked. T-Bone was properly fucked, physically, following the accident, without Al going to work on his mental health as well.

Regardless of his age and his wealth, T-Bone stayed true to the classic biker's uniform. Denim was his choice of material, as opposed to the more common leather that the younger generation chose these days, while his long white hair and handlebar moustache completed the image. His skin was rough and extensively scarred, and his blue eyes sparkled in the low light of the office as he returned to his desk carrying a thick envelope. He sat down; leaned forward and handed it to Tubbs. Foxy's jade ring glistened on the pinky finger of his left hand, reminding T-Bone at once of what he'd lost.

"Here's half of it. The other half's already been transferred, as per usual, ok?

"Thanks," said Tubbs as the Scouser's orthopaedic shoe flashed in front of his eyes.

As he placed the cash in his pocket, he thought about how small the bundle appeared, after so long collecting the blood money. He remembered the first time he was handed such an amount. He'd never seen so much money and didn't know what to do with it. He rose slowly as the pain from his fresh scars ripped through his leg once again. He winced.

"What's with the Olbas oil?"

T-Bone beckoned Tubbs to follow and handed him a flannel.

"You'll need that," he said and led the way towards the door at the back of the office, which opened onto a narrow, dimly-lit corridor. At the end of the passage, T-Bone slowly opened the door to a small, dark cell, with no windows. The odour intensified with every step and both men's eyes were soon streaming into the hand towels held tightly over their noses and mouths.

T-Bone turned on the lights. Sat on a chair in the far corner was a man – his hands, his legs and his midriff tied tightly with red rope. His head was placed in some kind of vice, which stopped him from moving anything except his eyes. His mouth was gagged but it was his eyes that demanded almost all of Tubbs's attention. By using an excessive amount of industrial tape and some laboratory clamps, T-Bone had managed to stop the man from blinking. But that was the least of his problems at this time, as his eyeballs had been burned into his skull after four days of continuous torture. He squirmed. Tried to scream. Could barely do either. Directly above his eyes, held in place by some kind of adapted microphone stand and dripping slowly and continuously into the eye sockets, making light work of his irises and retinas, were two industrial-sized bottles of Olbas Oil.

"Chinese torture with a modern twist," explained T-Bone proudly.

Tubbs turned his back and quick-stepped back to the office. Maybe T-Bone's body – his shell – was old and feeble, but his mind was as merciless as ever.

POSITION VACANT

THE MARK gone, the money pocketed, Gimp smoked and watched Vexl slowly roll a crisp twenty between his thumb and forefinger and hoover up a fat line of phet from the kitchen table. Throwing his dreads back in response to the back-draft that just blew up his nostrils and exploded in his brain, Vexl waited for the rush to subside before passing the note to his friend, so he could follow suit. Gimp took the nosepipe. Froze. The last thing he wanted was a line. What he *really* needed was sleep. A nice long kip in a nice cosy bed. Vexl noticed his hesitation, and looked over the table at him.

"Eh dere, bad bwoi, watcha waitin' for? We nyah got all day, mon…" and like the weak man that he was, Gimp plunged towards the tabletop, and did what he had to do. After the crystals had burned his sinuses to fuck and back, and the familiar taste of bloody metal appeared in the back of his throat, Gimp lit another Marlboro as Vexl went to work building a six-skinner to tide them over. In went the baccy, the skunk and a crushed-up slimming pill. The clock on the oven flashed 11:03. *No more!* pleaded Gimp's inner wise man. And without word he got to his feet, left the kitchen and ran upstairs to the relative sanctuary of Vicky Rosé's bedroom.

In super-slo-mo, Vexl watched him go, but his brain-mouth-coordination was so devastated by now that he failed to utter a single word. He knew exactly where Gimp was going and right on cue, Vicky's headboard started banging, proving once again that Gimpmon was no fan of foreplay. Vexl didn't like the fact that Gimp and Vicky were in some kind of relationship, after all the first rule of Pimp School is 'never sleep with the girls that work for you', but he didn't want to deny the little man a little pleasure either. He was such an odd-looking bastard, he'd struggle to get any kind of lovin' unless he knew Vicky. A freak show started to take shape inside Vexl's head – Gimp the dwarf riding Vicky the putrid prossie with more zeal than Frankie Dettori careering for the finish line on the back of Sergeant Cecil. The banging, the uh-uh-uh-ing and the chemicals coursing through his system hypnotised Vexl and as a result he didn't even notice Miss Scarlett when she entered the kitchen and filled the kettle.

"You wanna cup o' tea, Vex?" asked the young hooker, shaking Vexl from his x-rated subconscious. He turned to look at her. Shook his head slowly. Silently. Appreciated her cheap, tacky beauty, and then turned his attention back to the huge spliff that lay before him. After years of industrial-scale drug abuse the speed didn't have the usual effect on him any more – namely non-stop chattering and verbal *diarrhoea. These days, it slowed everything down to a crawl.*

He rolled the carrot and licked the gum, inserted the roach and lit her up, before turning his attention once again to Miss Scarlett, who was facing away from him, stirring her cuppa and staring out the window. She was nineteen. Blonde. Her eyes as blue as her profession. Miss Scarlett had been here for the past three months, after Vexl had found her in the usual way – outside Cardiff Central train station, lost and alone and looking for something, someone to offer her some hope. With little experience she'd proved herself to be very professional and fully deserved her promotion to Vexl's other brothel, located in Cardiff's Riverside area, a short walk from the centre of town.

As she turned on the radio and started humming along to some shit tune, Vexl considered how happy he was with his current stable. It was the perfect size at present – five girls working from two houses in two towns – which allowed him to manage the girls and make enough money to pay the rent and keep himself high. In Vexl's opinion, bigger stables only caused problems, and with his mind almost constantly shot to pieces, that was the last thing he needed.

"So you got anyone lined up to take my place then, Vex?"

"Yeah, nana, I gotta sweet young t'ing a waitin'," lied Vexl. Of course he didn't have anyone lined up. Never did. He rarely planned anything. He lived – survived – from day to day. Always had. Always would. Suddenly, he remembered the spliff that had long stopped smoking in the ashtray, so he picked it up, put it to his mouth and lit it again, filling the room with stinking purple smoke. Through the haze, he studied and appreciated Miss Scarlett once again. If only he could get a hard-on, he wouldn't mind laying that pipe and breaking the first rule right here, right now, on the kitchen table. But, along with the majority of his brain cells, his boner had long left the building.

"Here's that eighty from last night," said Miss Scarlett, taking the spliff from Vexl before it went out again. "Did you catch him on the way out?"

"Ah yeah," smiled Vexl.

"Did you like him? I chose him 'specially for you… sort of like a thank you…"

Thanks for what, Vexl didn't know, because he treated his girls like shit. But he did appreciate her enthusiasm. That would be a sign of weakness. If only every whore was as contented, professional and easy-going as this one, then life would indeed be a breeze. Some girls hated parting with their hard-earned cash – that's why Vexl carried his knives. A little threat now and again, a reminder of who's boss, was an effective way of keeping order, and he wasn't scared to use them either. In fact, he loved slicing through skin.

Upstairs, the headboard banged wildly for ten seconds or so as Gimp, at last, shot his measly load while screaming *OHHHHHHH MOMMMMMMMA* in his high-pitched voice. As normality returned to the kitchen, Vexl thought about

Vicky for a second or two. In complete contrast to Scarlett sitting opposite him, she was a prime example of an angry, sad, and fucked off working girl. The fact that she had Aids was a defining factor of course, which in turn led her down a path of self-destruction and self-loathing. She looked rough as fuck, had done for years, but her insides were rotting by now as well as her outer shell, thanks to the steady stream of diet pills and sedatives she popped on a daily basis, and not forgetting her other, legitimate, medication. She was skeletal now. A bag of bones. With yellow teeth and bad skin. She was always complaining about the way Vexl treated her, but who else would have her? Who else would employ her? And she fuckin' knew that, deep down. The ungrateful cunt. Vexl was always amazed when she got a punter, but there was no denying that she must do something right as she had a long list of suckers that returned to her habitually. Fuck knows what she did to them. But whatever it was, it worked.

"When we goin' to Kaadiff then, Vex?"

"A'soon as dis pair are done de bashment…" explained Vexl, although Scarlett barely understood a word he said.

"Well, I'm ready to go when you is."

"Cool."

And as the spliff passed between them once again, Gimp and Vicky appeared in the kitchen – Gimp grinning and Vicky's bones trembling under her translucent skin.

"Is 'at what I thinks it is?" she asked.

"'Ere you are, luv," said Miss Scarlett, as she passed her the stump. Vicky pulled hard on the cardboard, sucking the smoke deep down into her lungs, which made the shakes disappear at once.

"Ahhhhhhhhh," she sighed as she blew the smoke towards the closed window. "Who wants a cuppa then?"

"Too right, dolly, milk three sugars, innit?" said Gimp.

"Nah time, mon, we best be shiftin'…" piped Vexl, as he stood up for the first time in ages. His head spun. His legs buckled. But he held it together. Just.

"You off already, is it? Fackin 'ell, you could 'ave told me… come 'ere, luv," said Vicky, as she pulled Scarlett in for a goodbye hug. After leaving a handful of pills on the table, Vexl and Gimp left them to it and headed for the car. As they stepped into the vehicle, Vexl asked his partner:

"D'yuh gyet da loot, mon?"

"I always get ve loot, bruvva," answered Gimp, lighting another red cherry and watching Miss Scarlett leave the house, pulling her whole life on two wheels behind her in a bright pink suitcase.

The brothel in Barry was little more than a test centre, with Vexl offering the new and inexperienced girls a chance to hone their skills there before moving them on to Cardiff and the capital's more selective clientele.

Miss Scarlett's swift advancement did mean one small problem for Vexl though, namely that he needed to fill her room as soon as poss. And Vexl fully intended to return to Barry before the end of the day with a new mare – ideally of a similar pedigree to Miss Scarlett if that was at all possible.

Without once breaking the speed limit, Gimp drove to number 12 Merches Garden, which had a pretty good view of the Millennium Stadium if you craned your neck out the Velux window at a hideously impossible angle. He parked the car and led the way – Vexl by his side, Scarlett a few yards behind. Vexl opened the door with his keys and soon they were sat in the kitchen at the back of the house. Déjà vu. The most noticeable thing on entering the house was the noise – dull thudding and raised voices proclaiming their satisfaction in the traditional way – followed by the smell, which was a heady combination of sweat, spunk and a slight hint of seafood.

Vexl smiled as he listened. It was just past mid-day and already the girls were busy. This branch of his small empire was more profitable than the one in Barry and Miss Scarlett would have to work a bit harder here than she was used to. But Vexl already knew that she'd be up for the challenge.

Gimp lit a fag, offered the pack around, and lit the one between Scarlett's full red lips; while Vexl went to work crushing another couple of pills. Just as Gimp snorted his, they heard footsteps descending the stairs, followed by some muffled voices and the front door opening, then closing as another happy punter left the premises, his gonads a little lighter than when he arrived.

Leanne appeared in the kitchen almost at once, wearing nothing more than a purple robe, which was undone when she arrived. She covered herself, before speaking.

"All right, I didn't hear you come in," she sat down on the last empty chair, lit a Marlboro which she took without asking from Gimp's packet. Leanne was this brothel's senior girl. She was twenty-six and had worked for Vexl for six years. Her body was toned, her skin taut and nicely tanned, while her red hair cascaded over her shoulders. She pretty much ran things here on Vexl's behalf.

Through his shades, Gimp stared at her. Studied the contours of her semi-exposed body.

"Dis be Miss Scarlad," said Vexl.

"Stand up girlie and lemme take a look at you," she barked in an accent that can only be described as Vexlesque, and Scarlett did exactly as she was told. Leanne looked her slowly up and down. "Turn 'round now." And again, that's exactly what she did. "Mmmmmmmmmm!" moaned Leanne, which is exactly what both Vexl and Gimp thought as they sat there staring at her perfect behind. "Come wit' me, missy. I take you to yo' room…"

Vexl got to his feet, without having to adjust his manhood,

while Gimp got up like a thirteen-year-old boy at a sixth-form swimming gala.

"Where to?" asked Gimp, when they were both safely back in the car.

"Central," came the reply. And after finding a space in short term parking right in front of the train station, they popped a pill each, lit a fag and sat back in the afternoon sun to watch and to wait.

NO LEG TO STAND ON

RICHIE HELD her hand as tightly as a terrified child. Petra felt the sweat on her soon-to-be ex-boyfriend's palm and longed for him to let go. She didn't even want him to come with her this morning, but he heard her get up and insisted on walking her to the point of no return.

Although the sun was shining today on Merthyr Tydfil, the inside of the bus station shivered perpetually thanks to the structure's solid concrete shell and the draft that swirled continuously. Petra regretted not wearing more clothes. That was her nature and she wouldn't change for anyone. Wearing a belt for a skirt, a tight white vest, a fake pair of light brown UGG boots, straight off the back of a lorry, with her long blonde ringlets cascading over her creamy shoulders; Petra was a walking-talking-teenage wet dream.

In her other hand, the one that wasn't being squeezed by Richie's clammy claw, she dragged a little pink suitcase on wheels. Petra was running away. Not from anything or anyone in particular, but after losing her parents about a year ago in a fire started accidentally by her, she simply couldn't go on living in her home town anymore. She'd been christened 'the parent trap' by some, 'candle killer' by others and 'death doll' as well. Apart from Richie, she didn't have any close friends anymore, and she didn't really want Richie's friendship any longer either.

Of course, he'd been very good to her during the hell that was the aftermath of her parents' death and gave her shelter in his little bedsit above the chippy in the centre of town, but the time had come for Petra to move on, before she lost it completely and followed her parents to the afterlife, doggie-paddling down the River Styx. Their voices echoed off every building, every tree and every face in town, while the nightmares haunted her every time she closed her eyes.

Although she was running away, she did have a plan. Well, maybe not a plan per se, but a dream. A silly dream that would probably never be fulfilled.

"This is it then," Richie sighed, as the Cardiff bus pulled into the station. He couldn't even look at her.

"Don' look so gutted, babes, I'm only goin' to Cardeff. And anyway, youah followin' me down afta you finesh youah apprenticeship, 'n ew."

Richie looked up from the floor and managed a sad little smile. He knew this would be the last time he saw her and was devastated about that. It wasn't every day you bagged a chick like Petra. Especially in Merthyr, where most of the girls look like pre-ops with a leopard print fixation.

"Just be careful, ok. There are some seriously bad cunts down Cardiff…"

"There ah bad cunts everywhere, Rich, and youah speaken to public enemy numba one, by ere."

"Just… you knows…"

"Yeah, I knows. And anyway, Stacey'll look afta me til I get on my feet, like."

Stacey was Petra's imaginary friend. Someone she'd invented to soothe Richie's concerns. She'd even made up an address and a phone number and claimed that she'd be staying with her for the first few weeks until she found her own place or whatever. In truth, Petra had no idea what she'd do when she got to Cardiff.

The driver took her case and placed it in the boot of the bus.

"I loves you, Pet," blurted Richie. Petra groaned in response. She hated it when people abbreviated her name. She *was* an animal, of that there was no denying, but she was far from being tame.

"See ya, Rich," was her cold farewell. She didn't love him. She hadn't exactly been faithful to him either. Monogamy was something she was keeping for *the one*, not just *any*one.

Petra got on the bus and found a seat about halfway down. The bus was pretty empty. A man sat on the back seat, sipping Special Brew and mumbling to himself. Their eyes met for a split-second before Petra took her seat and watched Richie walk out of the station and out of her life. She felt a slight pang of regret, but it didn't last long. She reached in her fake Burberry handbag and pulled out her book as the bus left the station. The hard-backed tome was called *Lion Boy*. It was a fantasy novel about a boy who was fluent in a language spoken by every cat in the world – domestic and wild. Petra loved cats, and missed little Marley almost as much as her parents. She hadn't seen the little black and white furball since the night of the fire and didn't know if she'd died in the flames or ran away. She shook her head to relieve the sadness, but when she returned to the present, she was faced by something equally bad, if not worse.

To her left, in the seat opposite and across the aisle, Mr Special Brew sat, tinny in hand, staring at her through glassy, bloodshot eyes. Up close, in his heavily-stained duffel coat and grotty suit, he looked like a flasher, as well as a tramp. And right on cue, he undid his zipper, pulled his todger out and started stroking it with his spare hand, working up a feeble chub without ever truly threatening to achieve full wood.

"Wrap your legsh aroond thish, dollfashe!" he slurred.

"Fuck off back to youah seat..." Petra hissed. "...before I scream an' get you chucked off." She wasn't scared of him. She'd dealt with twats like this plenty of times before. Petra usually enjoyed being the object of desire, that's why she tended to dress like a slut, although there were some obvious downsides.

"Come on, dolly, I won't bite cha," smiled the wanker.

He leaned across the aisle with his lifeless member hanging

out the front of his trousers like the trunk of a soft toy, he lunged towards her. But Petra smacked him with the spine of her book – the perfect backhand that smashed his nose and sent the gippo flying back across the aisle and into the seat opposite. With both hands holding his snout but not succeeding in stopping the flow of blood, Petra rose to her full height, spitting her whispered directions at him; her eyes wide open and the adrenalin coursing through her body.

"Gerrup you stinken twat and fuck off back there where no one can smell you!"

Slowly, the wounded animal dragged himself to the back of the bus, leaving a trail of blood. Petra calmly wiped the book cover on the back of a chair and sat down again, although she found it hard to concentrate on the story for a few minutes as her heart rate struggled to regain its natural rhythm.

The coach wound its way slowly down the valleys towards Cardiff, turning a half-hour journey into one approaching ninety minutes due to all the diversions. Petra read, dozed, looked over her shoulder and daydreamed, and with the sun still blazing high in the sky above, she looked out the window just as the coach took off over Gabalfa flyover. She could see Llandaf Cathedral's steeple rising in the middle distance, beyond the high rises, while Tesco Extra and the Mynachdy estate claimed the foreground. She could recall visiting the cathedral with her parents when she was little. Not that they were religious in any way. And she couldn't actually remember anything about the church itself either, just the tasty chips and sweet and sour sauce she had from the Chinese takeaway in the nearby village.

Her heart started racing as the bus continued down North Road, past the Porsche garage, the army of students that had colonised the area, before at last reaching the civic centre and the CBD. She stared at the castle, gawped at the hordes and the traffic. She was close now, she knew that. But close to what? She didn't have a clue.

On reaching journey's end, Petra looked towards the back of the bus as she gathered her pack and saw her attacker snoring and dribbling in equal measures, his nose a volcano of crimson, lava flowing down his chin. She stepped off, collected her suitcase and headed for the nearby train station and the tourist information office she remembered seeing there the last time she came to Cardiff. But when she reached the lobby, the tourist office was nowhere to be seen.

She turned and left the station once again, through the main exit, with the intention of asking the first copper she saw for the nearest tourist office so she could find somewhere to stay.

But first she needed a fag. She leant on the wall in the cool shade, and reached for her L&Bs. She lit up, inhaled deeply and closed her eyes for a few seconds.

"Gorra spare one o' 'em, spa?" Petra looked left, then right. Saw no one. "Down 'ere, spa!" the voice exclaimed. And Petra looked down to see another tramp, this one *literally* legless and dragging himself around the piazza on some kind of skateboard with his gloved hands. He smiled broadly, teeth crooked and brown. Petra pulled a fag from her packet and dangled it in front of him.

"You can 'ave this, no problem. But first you gorra 'elp us with summin', ok?"

"Name it, spa."

"It's quite simple. All I need to know is where the nearest 'ostel is – you know, YHA or backpacka type place – and how to get there. Can ew 'elp me?"

"Fuck yes!" beamed Stumpy, lifting himself up to grab the cigarette from her grasp, like a stunted seal at a sea centre, but Petra was too quick and he swatted the air and almost fell off his board.

"Uh-uh-uh! Tell me first, and then you gets youah reward."

"All right, spa, keep sveed! It's a piece of piss. See that massive pub-type building over there, beyond Bee Kay," he said, pointing towards GW's, one of the few original buildings to survive the city centre's severe urban renewal project. "Take a left down the alley just before you gets there and the entrance is about fifty yards down on your right. The hostel's above the shops on St Mary Street see, that's why the entrance is round the back like…"

"Thanks!" said Petra, dropping the ciggy into his lap and walking away.

Gimp got within twenty yards of the blonde girl before Val Stumps started talking to her. He stopped walking and watched. Val was a bit of a local legend who usually worked with his partner, Lord Snowdon. Drunk as fuck was their default setting. In fact, the only time they were ever sober was when they didn't have any funds. Like right now. There was no sign of Snowdon today though, but that didn't surprise Gimp. They were pulling a scam to get some cash, and when Val pointed towards GW's Gimp knew at once what was about to unfold. So when the blonde started walking away, Gimp followed her at a safe distance, pulling his mobile from his pocket to call Vex.

"Ya mon?"

"Take ve motuh to ve uvva end ov ve lane…" Gimp ordered.

"What lane, mon?"

"Ve one by GW's comes out by ve Prince ov Wales, you know."

"Ya mon." They made a good team at times, especially when hunting. However, Gimp had no idea what he was going to do now – how he was going to get the girl out of Snowdon's grasp and into the car, that is – but he was sure that he'd think of something. He usually did.

Petra hesitated at the top of the lane and doubted the legless layabout for a split-second. But, after taking one last drag on her fag, off she went in the hope that he wasn't lying. Why would he?

Some hundred yards down the alley, she realised that she'd been well and truly done. There was no hostel. Just some wheelie bins, a few fire exits and a man-mountain holding a huge hunting knife a few inches from her face.

She stared at the lumbering colossus. Cursed herself for being so naïve. So gullable. So *valleys*. She'd never seen such a specimen before. He stood closer to seven feet than six, and weighed at least twenty stone. The knife, although large by anyone else's standards, looked like a Fisher Price toy in his paw. Petra smiled in the hope that she might confuse him. He did look easily confused, after all; like an ex-heavyweight boxer who's taken one too many knocks to the head. On seeing her smile, he grunted; which took Petra by surprise and wiped the smirk from her face. The grunting then became a growl, followed by a wild stab which Petra managed to dodge, thanks mainly to the fact that Snowdon moved slower than the mountain he was named after. Petra regained her balance, but before her legs could whisk her away, the hulk had hold of her hair. She screamed, kicked, spat and hoped that he wanted nothing more than her money.

"Take my bag!" she bellowed, staring at the blade the behemoth held a few inches from her face.

As expected, Gimp saw Snowdon step out from behind a wheelie bin just as blondie walked by. The big bastard was about as dynamic as a dinosaur bone, but after a bit of a stand-off, he somehow managed to grab her by the hair. This reflected badly on the blonde, but Gimp would give her the benefit of the doubt, as he had to admit that Snowdon, regardless of his limited intellect and restricted mobility, was one terrifying looking brute, especially the first time you clocked him.

Gimp saw Vexl's car pull up at the far end of the alley and started running as fast as he could towards the beauty and the beast...

Petra stopped squirming and swallowed hard. The knuckles of her hand that still held the suitcase had turned white. She considered swinging it at her captor, but settled for praying for a miracle; or failing that, some help.

And as if Loki himself had heard her plea, a midget appeared from the ether, screaming and sprinting towards them. He flew down the alley, grabbed her by the wrist and whisked her away in a blur of heavy breathing, leaving the giant rooted to the spot, holding nothing but a clump of hair in his huge hand.

Within seconds, Gimp was stuffing the blonde into the back seat of the car and slamming the door behind them so that Vexl could drive off. He had no idea what had just happened, how he'd managed to liberate the lovely. He looked back up the alley at a tragi-comic scene: Lord Snowdon, hair in one hand, knife in the other, being berated by Val Stumps from his position close to the ground; the legless alky's face flushed positively crimson and filled with desperation and despair.

As Vexl pulled a three-pointer and joined the steady flow of traffic heading towards Riverside, Petra looked at her pint-sized saviour, sat beside her, staring and smiling like a fuckwit. She smiled back before, which is when she saw the state of the driver. Now if the dwarf beside her looked weird, the mess behind the wheel was monstrous. With his thick dreads and translucent skin, he looked like a Rasta Goth or something.

She turned once again towards her redeemer, but before she could ask him what was going on, both men started laughing.

DISGRACELAND

F ROM THE air, the huge country pile looked a little like the White House in Washington DC – with more curves than the Playboy Mansion, tall Italianate pillars at the front and windows reaching from floor to ceiling. But, unlike the president of the free world's pad, this white house had a 25-metre heated outdoor swimming pool at its back, stretching towards the landscaped grounds, fishing lake, stables, driving range and the rest of the estate's many outbuildings.

This morning, with the early sun peeping lazily over the ancient oaks and the majority of those who lived here still sleeping off the previous evening's excesses, one lone star was taking a swim. In the clear blue water of the pool, Luca Parenti swam as he did at every opportunity when he was home on the farm, free from the rigours of life as one of Italy's leading exponents of psychedelic-folk-rock. As he struggled somewhat to complete the last of this morning's forty lengths, his hands finally touched the smooth pool side. At once, his feet touched the floor of the shallow end and his black curly hair rose out of the water so that he could recapture his regular breathing pattern.

He regretted smoking that half a joint between his earlier yoga session and his swim, but it was too late to do anything about that now. His lungs burned and the mucus was thick in his throat. He spat. Held his forefinger to his right nostril. Blew through the left. Repeated on the other side. Then he walked slowly through the shallows and climbed out of the pool as he felt the early morning sun caressing his already almond skin.

As he dripped on the mock-marble paving, he stretched his body, nice and slow, before placing his Aviators on his hooked nose and easing into the bubbling whirlpool. As the jets tickled his testes and gently kneaded his toned muscles, he reached for the large iced glass of freshly squeezed OJ. He took a swig, placed it back in the shadows, dried his hands on his towel and grabbed the stinking, skunk-filled stump from the ashtray. He lay back, closed his eyes and listened to the birds serenade each other in the trees that surrounded his sanctuary. He opened them again and watched the wispy clouds sail slowly. He'd miss this place a lot over the coming week, during his latest tour of Italy, promoting his new LP, *Anima Dannata*, a collection of stripped-back acoustic songs in Italian, English and Welsh. And although he'd much rather stay here – swimming, riding and maybe recording some new material – he knew that these things had to be done, in order to maintain the lifestyle he'd long become accustomed to living.

After a long soak in the tub, and after the spliff and the juice had disappeared, Luca left the Jacuzzi, put on his robe and ambled back to his home's huge kitchen.

He opened the Smeg fridge, reached for the jug of fresh orange juice to replenish his glass and quietly appreciated his good fortune. Glass in hand, he turned to the coffee machine and as the water started to bubble beside him on the granite worktop, he watched two of his horses in the field closest to the house and Ceredigion Bay glistening beyond in the early sunlight.

While pouring the coffee he noticed the pink envelope addressed to him lying on top of the pile of post that had accumulated over the last few days. He opened the envelope with the long strong nail of his forefinger, and stared for some time at the photo that dropped into his hand. He swallowed some sweet black coffee. Stared some more. Twins. Identical. Eighteen. Possibly twenty. No more. Beautiful. Absolutely beautiful. He appreciated their combined beauty – their olive skin, deep dark eyes, long wavy black hair and blowjob lips that promised so much pleasure – before turning his attention to the accompanying letter.

Ciao Luca,

I love you. Carolina, me sistr, she also love you. We are twin. Identical twin, yes? We 19 old. We live on farm (like yu!) in region of Umbria, centrale Italia. You music make us happy. So happy. You so very hansum, with curl hair and Italian skin. So brown. If you ever visit Perugia, you must come us. We live 1 hour only from Perugia, very easy. You can stay with us, no problem. You welcome. We make yu happy. Very happy. You will lick us make happy. Our heart belong to you...

Ti voglio bene.

Baci, Caterina e Carolina Maldini

PS – you lick photo us?

I lick it very much! thought Luca, as he stared once again at the photo. Was it too late to fly them over for tonight's party? Of course it was. Darren, his manager, wouldn't have any of that. No way. So he placed the letter and photo in his dressing gown pocket and smiled as he remembered that Perugia was definitely on the coming week's itinerary.

He received fan mail in some form on an almost daily basis, but they didn't usually include such beauties. Begging letters? Check. Old women? Check. Gays? Check. Weirdos? Check. Offering all sorts of wrongness and saying some of the strangest things. He kept them all – the good ones anyway – in a scrapbook, and got them out whenever the subject came up. Never failed to give everyone a good chuckle. One thing Luca had never understood was why most of the letters he received were written in English, when he was a fluent Italian speaker, but he appreciated the effort and, without a doubt, the pigeon

English added plenty of comedy. As a rule, he never took them seriously, but these twins demanded his attention, and Luca fully intended on paying them a visit in the coming week. Or even better, inviting them to the Perugia show and his hotel suite afterwards...

He had a lot to be grateful for, but the thanks mainly lay at his late parents' feet. Ernesto and Tita Parenti moved from Florence to Wales at the end of the Second World War and established the first ice cream parlour in Llandysul, a tiny rural town in Ceredigion's ass-crack, in 1951. Their produce proved to be very popular and before long *Gelato Parenti* had outgrown Llandysul and started spreading all over the principality, drawing the attention of the large corporations. The proud couple refused to sell their secret during their lifetime, but the flourishing business made them very rich and paid for Luca's private education at Cardiff's prestigious Cathedral School. But tragedy struck while Luca and his friends were in Ibiza celebrating the end of their A-level exams when news arrived of his parents' death in a helicopter accident near their country estate in Ceredigion, after their chopper went down on Penbryn beach, a few hundred yards from their home.

And just like that, Luca owned the lot, and after a few months of serious moping, he got busy and started establishing his empire and fulfilling all his dreams. Firstly, he sold his parents' secret recipe to the highest bidder – Haagen Dazs as it happens – for £2million. And although doing so haunted him for many years, he knew deep down that his parents would have been ok with his decision as it guaranteed his financial security forever, and all they were ever interested in was his wellbeing.

He used the cash to turn his parents' Bryncelyn Estate into Disgraceland – converting the cart-house into a studio where he could record his music; the large barn into an industrial scale ganja plantation; and filling the stable with a battalion of stallions so that he could go riding whenever he felt like it. The swimming pool, driving range, fishing lake and tepees were added a little later, following the success of his debut album, *Dio Celtico*, which sold more than a million copies in Italy alone in the first month after its release.

Regardless of his ongoing musical success, Luca and his associates' main income came from the ganja growing operation.

The profit made by the plantation allowed Luca to employ his closest friends as full-time staff. Ten people lived permanently on the estate and Luca had met every one of them – except for Blod, the gardening guru – during his time at the Cathedral School in Cardiff. He employed three full-time gardeners who looked after the grounds as well as helping Blod out in the grow room; a producer and engineer who hardly ever left the studio; two others who looked after the horses and stables; one in charge of security; and his manager, Darren.

Due to the nature of the estate's main industry, visitor access to Disgraceland was restricted, and apart from the parties that took place maybe once a month, this tight-knit group of friends was concerned almost entirely with their business. Of course, there was a steady stream of visiting girls and musicians, but no one was allowed to stay for too long and no one would dare whisper a word about what really went on in the barn. After all, doing so could ruin their lives and all they'd ever worked for.

Luca finished his homemade muesli – a speciality of Darren's, who trained as a chef before beginning to manage his friend – and fully appreciated his manager's many talents. Darren, of course, was much more that *just* a manager. He was a father figure, a brother, a cook, a bodyguard, promoter, mother, driver, agony aunt, procurer of magic potions, personal assistant and best friend. Everything that a modern day rock star needed – rolled into one person.

After placing his bowl and spoon in the dishwasher, Luca wrapped another couple of joints while listening to the news, and headed to his bedroom where he smoked a little, had a quick shower and got dressed, then left the house lighting a stump. The grandfather clock in the hall chimed for the ninth time as he closed the door behind him. The others would soon be getting up. But Luca didn't mind, he loved the peace and quiet of the early morning, when he had the whole place to himself, especially when the sun was shining like it was today.

The twins' faces flashed in front of his eyes and he smiled broadly in anticipation. He'd definitely invite them to stay with him when he played Perugia next week. And in the meantime he'd probably get laid tonight. That's what usually happened when he held a party anyway…

Ryan and Ronnie, two of the estate's most loveable horses, trotted over to say hello, so Luca reached in his pocket and gave them both a couple of sugar cubes. Within seconds, four more horses had appeared, and that's where Luca stood for a good five minutes, making small-talk with his equine acquaintances. After exhausting his sweet supply, Luca hurdled the fence and lead Ronnie to the stables where he gave him a quick comb, placed his favourite saddle on his back, jumped on and aimed his snout towards the sea.

Luca would do this every day – rain or shine – when he was at home. For Luca, the true meaning of freedom was riding Ronnie around Disgraceland's abundant acreage – through the trees, along the clifftops, down to the beach and back again.

On the way out of the stables, Luca and Ronnie bumped into Pennar, one of the stable managers, as he made his way shakily to his post, rather grey and looking forward to a strong coffee before starting his chores. But when he saw Luca, all thoughts of work went out the window.

"Give us a minute and I'll come with you," he said, and without waiting for a reply, he jumped the fence, led Ryan to the stables and within two ticks was out the front and ready to go. Pennar was by far the most experienced rider in Disgraceland, and he even used to compete in point-to-point races with some success before a nasty injury put paid to that particular hobby. He'd join Luca on his early morning trot at every opportunity and as a result they'd become very close friends. The rest of the entourage used the quads or the golf carts to get around the estate, except for Blod who liked a good walk, but Luca and Pennar favoured four legs and a personality over four wheels and some petrol.

They trotted and chatted as they went past the driving range and lake, before cantering through the trees which took them to the edge of the estate a little less than a mile away. There, at the edge of a steep cliff overlooking Penbryn Beach and Ceredigion Bay below, the steeds instinctively stopped so their riders could appreciate the view, as they always did, as long as it wasn't raining too heavily.

"How's your head then?" Asked Luca.

"Bit fuzzy. But there's no better way to clear a hangover than a bit of a gallop, is there…?"

"There is," smiled Luca as he produced a ready-rolled spliff from the pocket of his combat trousers, put it to his mouth and lit it. After inhaling deeply, he asked: "Did you hear the racket coming from the studio? Fuck knows what Blim and Sarge were up to…"

"I didn't as it happened. I pulled a full blown whitey after my third bong. Well embarrassing, I tell you."

"You were the lucky one, I reckon. They went on for hours. Fuckin' jokers. I thought they'd never stop."

"What time did they? Stop, that is."

"Around four, I think. But I had my headphones in well

before then, so I can't be sure. I went for a piss around ten past and they were quiet. But they'll be fucked today, I tell you."

"But not *too* fucked to do it all again tonight."

"Of course not. They're off their heads, those two. Anyway, what's the plan with tonight's party – the usual, or is there anything special lined up?"

"Fuck knows. Bit of this, bit of that, plenty of the other. I was thinking of trying to persuade Tubbs to come along. I saw Blod on the way to the stables and he told me he's picking up this arvo. I was gonna suggest he stays the night. Get fucked up. If he still does that shit. I mean, he's so quiet I don't think I've talked to him properly since school…" said Pennar, not that Tubbs had ever attended a private school, like Luca and the rest of his crew. It was true that Tubbs had met Luca and his boys when they were all in school – just not the *same* school. Through their shared love of all things herbal, these rapscallions met one sunny lunchtime near Blackweir bridge. And although as a rule Tubbs would avoid posh cunts at all costs, he learnt very quickly that the rich kids always had the best dope and their relationship developed from there.

"Business…" began Luca, before blowing five smoke rings in quick succession and continuing. "That's all the big man thinks about…"

"And his mam," added Pennar.

"True…"

"There's something really quite tragic about Tubbs. Some… I don't know… I can't quite put my finger on it… but…"

"Secrets and lies, man. Secrets and lies…"

"Seems to me he's constantly in hiding… but I s'ppose that goes hand in hand with his day job… but then again *we* don't hide…"

"Don't we?" asked Pennar.

"Well, just a little, maybe. But we're still quite social."

"More social than Tubbs, anyway…"

"Everyone's got something to hide though, haven't they?"

"Not me. What you see is what you get…"

"But what about that time you were caught 'inspecting'… was it Tony or Aloma… I forget which horse it was now…"

"Fuck off Luca, you know that isn't true!"

"Not one hundred per cent I don't," added Luca with a laugh. And before Pennar could get his grump on, he passed him the stump and said: "But you're right about inviting Tubbs tonight. It would do him good, I reckon. A few drinks, bit of a smoke, maybe even set him up with one of the girls…"

"Too right! That boy needs a shag, of that there is no doubt."

After a chuckle, a cough and a mouthful of cold water, the friends galloped back towards Disgraceland, the wind in their hair and their brains dragging behind. They came to a stop outside the barn where both dismounted and touched fists. Then Pennar led the horses back to the stables, while Luca went inside.

Luca opened the small side door of the barn using a key and code combination. The barn had no windows and was totally out of bounds to any visitor – even those, like Tubbs, who came here to buy their supplies – and every pick-up was prepared and handed over at Blod's office, which was annexed off the back of the barn. Luca stepped in and closed the door behind him, before breathing in the full green glory that grew before him. He closed his eyes and breathed as deeply as his dilapidated lungs would allow. Terry Wogan's voice could be heard on the radio in Blod's office at the other end of the barn, so Luca started walking in that direction, stopping now and again to sniff a bud or just gawp at the unnatural majesty that towered above him. The barn boasted a more sophisticated lighting system than most botanical gardens, while the watering system flushed the plants twice a day with all kinds of shit Luca had no real idea about. He left all the details to Blod. Luca placed his Ray-Bans on his nose once again, as the light in here was bright, while the sweat started skiing down his face and back, using his cheeks and shoulder-blades as moguls. Despite the discomfort, he stopped once again to inspect a gigantic sticky red bud. He sucked in its slight hint of minty freshness and smiled. This particular variety was called 'Big Bud' – Disgraceland's main strain these days. And although Blod liked to fuck around with cross-pollination, they were also forced to produce what the market demanded. And the market demanded extra strong skunk. Nothing else. Nothing fancy. And Big Bud fulfilled this criterion, and then some.

Blod's office was actually more like a mad professor's laboratory crossed with Carlos Castaneda's greenhouse. It was full of unbelievable cuttings and crossbreeds, fridges storing rare seeds and unique strains, as well as complex charts and detailed diagrams which meant nothing to anyone but Blod. It didn't take long for Luca to spot the wild white hair of the master, bent over the industrial scales in the far corner of the room, carefully weighing Tubbs's order.

Although Blod had weighed his orders for more than a decade, he'd never met the man himself. He often heard the boys talk about him, usually in hushed voices as if their old friend was some kind of phantom, but due to his own troubled history, Blod made every effort to avoid contact with the world outside the estate. Even ten years after 'the incident', the gardener didn't feel completely safe anywhere – not even here, at his place of work hidden away in Ceredigion's colon. He still half-expected someone to find him, but his past hadn't caught up with him… yet. The only things that interested him these days were his plants and his privacy. And for that reason he always got one of the others to deal with the customers, so that he could get on with the important stuff – namely growing and hiding.

"Alright, Blod," said Luca as he watched the professor adding two fistfuls of funk to the already bulging pile that lay on the scales.

"Good morning, Luca," came the reply, but not until Blod had finished his task and noted the weight.

"All good, Blod. How 'bout you? I just wanted to check that everything's under control cos I'm off to Italy tomorrow for a week or so…"

"Aye aye, no problem, Luca bach. You don't have to worry about a thing…"

In truth, Luca knew that before asking – the gardener's professionalism was absolute and his fingers were as green as his produce.

Of all of Disgraceland's staff, Blod was by far the biggest enigma. Luca met him for the first time some ten years ago, living wild in the woods surrounding the estate. To say that Luca had quite a shock to find this feral manbeast sleeping in a primitive, yet solid, shelter made of wood and moss, living on a diet of small mammals, fungi and fresh fruit within a few hundred yards of the mansion would be a bit of an understatement, but by now the original wooden structure has been turned into a simple, yet cosy, log cabin, surrounded by an Edenesque garden growing all sorts of vegetables. And although Luca still wondered from time to time why and how he came to be living there, he never pressurised Blod to reveal the truth. He was hiding from someone, that was pretty obvious, and he was more than welcome to hide here forever as far as Luca was concerned, especially once his skills as a ganja grower became apparent. Initially, Luca invited Blod to be a part of the estate's small team of gardeners, but it was pretty obvious almost from the start that his skills were wasted on planting bulbs and raking leaves. Within a few months of starting work in the grow room, Blod had turned a profitable business enterprise into a multi-million pound one.

"Coffee?" asked Blod, getting to his feet and wiping his sticky hands in his well-worn work jumper. "I need all the help I can get after last night's nonsense…"

"I'm alright thanks, but I'm on my way to the studio now. Everyone's complaining about the noise. I'm not really sure what happened, the studio's supposed to be fully soundproofed."

"Well it wasn't last night, that's for sure!"

"And there'll be more noise tonight, I'm afraid…"

"Oh yes, the party. My earplugs and Valium are at the ready!"

"Very good. I'll see you later then Blod, or maybe in a week or so…"

"Ok," came the absent reply, as the gardener turned his attention back to the scales.

Luca left through the back door, thus avoiding the grow-room's oppressive heat. He walked directly across the yard towards the cart-house and as he drew closer, he could see why the studio's soundproofing didn't work last night as the double doors of the entrance double doors were wide open.

Luca stepped into the studio and closed the doors behind him. He found Tim Blim, the engineer, and Sarge, the producer, both sound asleep on a leather sofa apiece in the middle of all the musical equipment and empty bottles. As well as being Luca's engineer, Blim was a multi-instrumentalist who had played on every one of his records so far, while Sarge was also much more that *just* a producer. One of them – Blim, if Luca had to make a guess – had chundered over Luca's favourite Fender Mustang and the Marshall amp it leaned against. The smell made him gag, so he pulled his shirt up over his nose and mouth.

Sarge was hugging his Hendrix white Fender Jazz Bass with pearl engraved fretboard. Thick drool flowed out the corner of his mouth with every breath he took.

Without waking them, Luca quietly sat on the leather revolving chair by the mixing desk and placed the cans on his head. He looked around the studio once again, shaking his head at the utter chaos. The sorry state of the Mustang made him want to batter Blim, but he didn't act on the impulse as he wasn't really that way inclined.

He turned his attention to the computer and searched for any new tracks recorded the previous night. He soon found a song called 'Kojak Blues' which was last saved at 04:05 that morning. Luca pressed play and listened. The bass was out of tune, the drums out of time, while the pedal-steel guitar wept, wailed and generally sounded as if it was mourning a recently departed loved one. The voices, however, sounded like two dogs on the way to slaughter, which fitted in well with the lyrics, which were all concerned with Disgraceland's resident pooch.

And right on cue, Kojak appeared from behind one of the sofas, tongue flapping, tail waggling, the bald patch on his head crying out for a little love. The old dog lay his head on Luca's lap and enjoyed the attention for a little while, and when the master got up to leave, he followed in the hope that he'd be given some breakfast, or at least some water, as his head too was banging after last night's session.

Before leaving, Luca set the track to repeat, turned up the volume and exacted a tiny bit of revenge on the two idiots who were still sound asleep. As the door closed behind them, Luca heard one of them get up in an attempt to stop the torture, before falling into the drum kit on his way to the desk.

They returned to the house through the garage – where Luca kept his small fleet of supercars – so that he could retrieve a few CDs from the Testarossa for the trip, and when he stepped out onto the drive he had quite a shock to see a police car parked there.

As it happened, Disgraceland had quite a few friends in the local police department who helped keep their business affairs private, for a reasonable monthly fee. But they never came in a marked car, which meant that this was more than a little worrying. Luca upped the pace, with Kojak doing likewise at his heel.

While stepping across the wide hallway towards the kitchen, Luca tried to remember if he'd cleared away the Rizlas and the bowl of skunk from the table, but when he arrived he was relieved to see the fat face of Detective Sergeant Carwyn Jenkins smiling back at him from beyond the heaped plate of pancakes, bacon and maple syrup that lay on the table before him. At the oven, cooking up the feast, stood Darren.

"Fuckin' hell, Carwyn, I shat it when I saw that car on the drive!"

"What car?" asked Darren.

"I came in a squad car today," explained Carwyn. "The Jag's in the garage having a service…"

"Pancake?"

"Go on then, Da'. One more won't hurt…"

"I wasn't asking you, you fat fuck!"

"Fuck you, Darren," came Carwyn's defensive reply. "And anyway, I'm not fat you ginger cunt!" He added, as both Luca and Darren looked at his bulging belly and mountainous manboobs.

"If you're not fat, you're definitely delusional!"

"Go on and laugh, you pair of cunts, but if I wasn't delusional I wouldn't be able to turn a blind eye to the naughtiness you boys get up to here, would I…?" Carwyn retorted, his mouth full of sweet-meaty delights and eyes looking at the thick brown envelope which lay on the kitchen table. This was the price Disgraceland had to pay to keep the local swine on side. Five grand a month. The money was split between the five members of the local drug squad, which in turn made sure that Disgraceland's business dealings were kept under wraps. Considering the size of the venture, they could have asked for double or triple the amount without much complaint, but everyone seemed quite happy with the arrangement. Especially Luca.

The singer sat at the table just as Darren placed a fresh pancake in front of him, although Luca hadn't answered his earlier question. By the time he'd added fresh lemon juice, sugar and some mint leaves, Darren joined them with a further two pancakes – one for him, the other for Carwyn.

The trio got stuck in and eat in silence for a little while, before Carwyn, once again, started talking.

"Party tonight then, is it boys?"

"Aye. You coming?"

"Too right! I've never missed one 'ave I? And I'm not going to start tonight. You off to Italy tomorrow, I hear…"

"I am. Bit of a promo tour. Nothing serious. What is it, Da', four gigs and a few TV appearances?"

"Something like that."

"Actually Carwyn, I've got a new box-set of my stuff around here somewhere. For your mam, like."

"Thanks, Luca. I appreciate it. You know how much she loves you…"

The first time Carwyn came to collect money from Disgraceland he mentioned in passing that his mam was a big fan of Luca's music, just to be polite and make some chit-chat in truth, but the singer, without any prompting, dug out a load of old tat – posters, mugs, CDs, T-shirts etc. – and signed the lot as a little extra sweetener. Luca even sang at the old girl's surprise sixtieth birthday party a few years ago, much to her delight.

Carwyn wiped his chins with a hanky. Burped.

"Before I go, do you boys need a little something to get the party started tonight?"

NO PAIN, NO GAIN

TUBBS OPENED his eyes and his thoughts turned straight to his mother. The only time that he wasn't haunted by her was when he'd meditate each morning. Apart from that brief hiatus, Foxy was never far from his thoughts. In fact, the rest of his waking life was borderline torturous – nothing but a steady stream of fragmented memories and an overwhelming desire to avenge her death. He'd been practising yoga for almost seven years now, having initially started after Luca mentioned that it helped him control his emotions, especially those connected to his parents' death. By now, he had mastered many aspects of the discipline, and found that it perfectly complemented the only martial art that he still practised regularly, namely the Lin Kuei style of kung fu, but no matter how good he was at yoga, he still wasn't quite in complete control of his emotions when it came to matters concerning his mam.

He rose slowly and steadily from the lotus position on the dark oak decking area in front of his home in Dinas Powys, a sleepy village tucked snugly between Cardiff's backside and Barry's shoulder blades, before stretching his muscles in a similar manner. His knee felt a little better this morning, although the wound was still pretty raw in places. The early morning sunshine tickled his bare toes as the birds in the trees chirped and chatted about who knows what. As he gave his glutes a good going-over he watched a pair of blue tits feasting on the food he'd hung out the previous afternoon, before one of the cheeky bastard squirrels that lived in the vicinity came along and scared them away.

He loved this place. T-Bone bought it as a gift for Foxy many years ago, although Tubbs couldn't remember his mentor ever visiting the place. T-Bone's life was left in tatters by her death as much as his own had been, so he couldn't blame him really, and although Tubbs found it hard sometimes to walk in her footsteps on a daily basis, he would never consider selling up and moving on – mainly because his mother's ashes were scattered under her favourite tree at the bottom of the garden and the greenhouses, which were full of various fruits and vegetables, served as some kind of living memorial to her passion for planting, cultivating and harvesting.

After finishing his warm-down, Tubbs left the squirrel to his breakfast and went in search of his own. He stepped off the deck and into his home – which was a simple, no frills, one-storey timber building, seemingly held together by ivy and consisting of two bedrooms, a large open-plan kitchen-diner-lounge area, a good-sized bathroom and not much else. The living area had a huge concertina door which opened onto the decking area and in the summer, with the doors wide open, the house almost became one with the garden beyond. He didn't have any neighbours, or at least, he couldn't *see* his neighbours from here as the garden was pretty extensive – at least an acre and a half, maybe two. A small stream snaked through the undergrowth, roughly halfway between the house and the greenhouses down the bottom, while a tall stone wall guarded his privacy even further. The mature grounds were given room to develop as nature intended and, apart from the three well-hidden greenhouses, the place was closer in truth to a nature reserve.

After five solid hours of sleep, Tubbs had woken as the sun peeped over the treetops and in through the windows of his bedroom. But thanks to the yoga session he was now ready to face the day. Without warning, the Scouser's face from the previous night flashed in front of his eyes, followed by the victim of T-Bone's torture, reminding him that no matter what, he would never be able to fully shake off the things he had done and seen, not even by avenging his mother's death. He leaned heavily on the kitchen worktop and breathed deeply until the vision burned away.

After feeding himself and five out of his six cats, Tubbs took a shower, dried carefully, covered his wounds with Preparation H and put on his gardening clothes – an old pair of comfy pants and a loose black vest, which showcased the galleries that were his thigh-thick arms. He filled a bowl with tuna for Victor, the one cat that hadn't yet eaten, before heading out to the garden once again. Tubbs knew exactly where he'd find the old feline: the same place he'd spend almost all of his time, lounging in the shade cast by Foxy's favourite tree. When she was alive, Victor was Foxy's favourite, and the only one still alive from her original menagerie. He was at least eighteen years old, which in cat years was pretty close to dead. He spent the majority of his time guarding the palm tree that Foxy and Tubbs planted when they initially moved here – the palm tree that Foxy had taken with her from the flat in Swansea, and the spot where Tubbs had scattered her ashes. The palm tree was something of a comfort blanket for Tubbs, especially when it would flower, and although he wasn't fluent in cat, he was pretty sure that Victor felt the same way.

As expected, Tubbs found Victor snoring in the sun beneath the palm tree. He bent down and stroked him gently, then laid the bowl on the floor so Victor could suck the oily fish down his ancient gullet. Although Victor had lost all of his teeth many years ago, there was nothing wrong with his appetite. Tubbs left him to it and walked to the greenhouses to water the crops. His interest in growing and nurturing plants started during the year after Foxy's death. Before that, he barely took any notice of the garden. She loved gardening. 'Pottering' she used to call it, which makes it sound as if she didn't really have a plan, or a clue. But that was far from being true. She was a master gardener, especially by the end, and her crops rarely failed. This garden's wild side was all her idea, while the greenhouses were a lesson in simplicity and effectiveness to anyone starting out. Due to her passion, Tubbs decided to continue her work, to look after her crops and maybe keep her spirit alive by doing so. That's what Tubbs told himself anyway, although the fact that he found a greenhouse full of collieweed growing wild also helped ignite his interest.

In the first greenhouse, Tubbs grew a variety of organic tomatoes, just as Foxy had done. A fantastical and familiar aroma filled the air as he drenched the plants with the hose. Tubbs breathed deeply before taking the water snake to the middle greenhouse, where he grew strawberries and grapes in a similar fashion – that is, without the use of chemicals. Once again, he drenched the plants before moving on to the third greenhouse.

He inspected the wide five-fingered leaves for mites and was relieved, as always, not to find any. The seaweed that covered the floor always seemed to do the trick. Tubbs recalled the carnage of his first attempt at growing a proper crop of collieweed, when he lost twenty mature plants to a plague of insects before he remembered what his mother used to fend off the bugs. Foxy would carpet the ground between her tomatoes and strawberries, and whatever else she might be growing, with seaweed from Sully Island. Tubbs had no idea where she learnt this trick, but since introducing the technique to his ganja-filled-greenhouse, he'd never had any problems.

Tubbs didn't like smoking the strong stuff anymore – the hydroponic skunk that Luca grew and that he sold to his contacts across the country – as the paranoia he felt when high was far too taxing for his fragile mind. He'd stopped smoking skunkweed at least six, maybe seven, years ago now.

These days, he'd fill his lungs from time to time with his homegrown organic grass, without polluting his pipe with tobacco or anything else.

Just as he was finishing up, Tubbs heard Boda's voice calling him from the top of the garden. He was the only other person who knew the security code that could open the gates. Without answering, Tubbs started jogging up to the house, through the thick foliage, for his meeting with the needle and ink.

Boda leaned on the side of the decking – portable tattoo kit lying by his feet, wearing the same clothes as when Tubbs saw him at the club some eight hours earlier. With his eyes hidden behind a pair of cheap sunglasses, Tubbs knew at once that Boda had not been home last night. As they shook hands, the sly smirk on Boda's face confirmed this.

Tubbs took the lead and headed for the kitchen. Coffee was needed. Lots of coffee.

"You're early," said Tubbs.

"Couldn't sleep," grinned Boda.

"Bullshit!"

"What?" came the reply as Boda tried in vain to fake some nonchalance.

"Nothing, but I can tell that you're dying to spill the beans…"

"Spill my load, more like!"

"So?"

"So what?"

"Don't be a twat. I know you're dying to tell me. I can tell by your just-had-a-fuck-face."

"Ok, ok. Follow me…" Boda stepped out of the kitchen onto the decking area and sat down by the round table. Tubbs did likewise. Boda then produced a ready-rolled cone from the pocket of his ripped-denim waistcoat, lit it up, sipped his coffee and started his story. Unfortunately for Tubbs there wasn't much to tell, as Boda's memory had been completely drowned by his old friend, Gentleman Jack.

"So all you can remember is waking up in her bed?"

"That's it."

"Nothing else?"

"Nada. Not a thing. What can I say? I was fuckin' wrecked up. You saw me!"

"But surely…"

"Surely *nothing*, Tubbs. These things sometimes happen…"

"Who was this girl anyway? I didn't see anyone with you at the club last night."

"You were only there for a few minutes, man!" Boda exclaimed defensively. The truth was he had no idea where he woke that morning nor who he woke up next to. She looked a bit rank from where he was lying, so he didn't hang around to find out. He put his clothes on quick smart and crept out of there as quietly as he could. Best case scenario – it was one of the barmaids from the club. Worst case scenario… he didn't even want to think about *that*.

"Now you sure you want to do this today?" Boda changed the subject. "I mean, yesterday's ink isn't even dry yet."

"Aye," Tubbs answered without a second's hesitation. "I'm fed up with the whole thing. You've been working on my leg for over three months now and I just want it finished so I can move on and maybe stop walking with a limp some time this year."

"Fair enough, but it's gonna hurt like fuck today. You have been warned, ok."

Tubbs went to change into a pair of shorts as Boda went through the lounge, where he put a CD by one of his favourite bands, Black Cesar, in the stereo, before turning his attention to the half-smoked spliff in his pocket as he awaited his friend's return. Boda used to run a tattoo parlour in Splott but with business slow and rent rising he decided to break with convention and start up a mobile service. This wasn't an original idea, but it was pretty unique in south Wales, and with his links to the Bandidos he was never short of work. In fact, due to the bikers' unquenchable appetite for ink, Boda's business was very much booming.

He inherited his skills from his father, Hawkeye – the artist responsible for the majority of the tattoos that decorated the ageing bodies of T-Bone and the older generation of Bandidos – as well as the shop, after the old man died in a motorcycle accident near Storey Arms some ten years ago. Boda had been practising the art under his father's watchful eye since he was thirteen and although he was only eighteen when Hawk died, Boda already had the necessary skills to run the business. He'd been working on Tubbs for the entirety of their adult lives. The small Mexican bandit silhouette on the top of Tubbs's right arm was the first of many, and he was still there to this day, among the myriad other images that Boda had etched permanently onto his husk.

Tubbs took his seat in the Lazyboy, pulled the right leg of his shorts right up to his groin and gritted his teeth. As per, Boda asked him the same question he always did before starting, although he knew the answer already.

"You want some anaesthetic today, Tubbs?" The question was a complete joke by now, and Tubbs just grinned at him. "Fine by me, but you knows I'll be concentrating on the knee today, and that's one of the worst…"

"Just get on with it, Bo." He insisted, before lying back, closing his eyes and concentrating on his yogic breathing technique as Boda's needle started to vibrate and buzz nearby.

Within an hour, Tubbs's knee was ripped to shreds once more and also hideously swollen. Boda carefully wiped the area and covered it with a thick layer of Preparation H.

"That's it for today, Tubbs. I can't do any more now. Too much blood, man."

Tubbs opened his eyes, looked at the mess. Grimaced.

"How long was I out for?"

"Only an hour," answered Boda as he lit the end of the joint and pulled hard on the roach. "Your knee's fucked, as you can see. I did say though, so no moaning alright. Put your feet up. You'll be ok tomorrow, I reckon…"

"No can do, Bo. I'm off west this arvo."

"Good luck with the driving."

"What d'you mean?"

"Try to stand up and we'll take it from there…" and as Tubbs struggled to get up from his chair, Boda smiled knowingly. "You're not going anywhere, man?"

"I've got to. No choice. I've got customers waiting. What you got planned?"

"Fuck all, as it happens. Sleeping. Chilling. Wanking. Not necessarily in that order."

"Change of plan. You're coming with me. As my chauffeur…"

"Luca's?"

"Yes. You up for it?"

"Fuckin' right!" And after a quick lunch consisting of bacon sarnies and more industrial strength coffee, Tubbs struggled to his car as Boda bounced alongside him, the hangover relegated to the back of his mind thanks to the excitement of visiting Disgraceland for the first time.

Within a couple of hours – including a piss stop and the most expensive plate of chips on the face of the earth for Boda at Pont Abraham service station – the VW Polo found itself west of Ffostrasol, slowly following a cack-covered tractor along some seriously narrow lanes. After a few miles, Boda finally lost his patience and overtook the tractor on a bit of a dodgy bend. Tubbs bellowed at him for being so careless, but soon mellowed as his friend was obviously so excited about visiting Luca Parenti's pad that he forgot the protocol for a split-second.

Boda had heard his friend talk about Disgraceland so many times over the years that images of fantastical proportions filled his head. And despite his ridiculous expectations, Boda wasn't disappointed when Tubbs directed him off the A487 towards Tresaith and the manor house's gated entrance.

As always, the portal to this magic place was locked, but after a quick word through the intercom, the gate opened and allowed them in. Boda slowly drove the Polo along the long winding driveway – gawping like a goldfish at the driving range, the fishing lake and the horses. T-Bone's gaff was pretty impressive, but Disgraceland blew his fucking mind.

Tubbs would usually go directly to the barn when coming to collect, but with Boda twitching and grinning by his side he knew that today's visit would be rather different from the norm, even before he saw Luca step out of the house and onto the driveway. He smiled broadly on seeing Tubbs and took a long drag on the joint that hung from the corner of his mouth as the big man battled his way out of the passenger seat.

"Yeeeeeeeeeeeeeeeeeeeees Tuuuuuuuubbs!" he exclaimed, shaking hands. "How's it going, all good I hope…"

"Not bad, Luca, apart from…"

"What?"

"Nothing. Forget it."

"Fuck off man, what's up?" And as Tubbs realised that Luca wasn't going to let this one slide, he carefully lifted his trouser-leg to show him the mess.

"Jeeezus!" Luca exclaimed, averting his eyes from the bloody pulp that was Tubbs's knee, and clocking Boda for the first time.

"Hey," he said with a smile, before turning back to Tubbs. "Who's this?"

"My chauffeur for the day and the bastard responsible for this…"

"Boda," said Boda, as he stepped towards Luca extending his hand while trying to act blasé and failing miserably. Not that Boda was a fan of his music or anything, but sharing breathing space with someone as clearly comfortable with his success and fame could make the coolest of cats feel a bit hot under the collar.

"Yo Bo! Top name. Top beard too…" and they shook hands before Luca offered him the spliff. "Ok, before you go on down to the barn to take care of business, I want to invite you both to tonight's party…"

"Sweet!" answered Boda, although the look on Tubbs's face wasn't so saccharine.

"Exactly," said Luca with a smile. "It's a sort of farewell party for me. Although I'm only off for a week. To Italy. Mini tour. Anyway. Nothing major. Just a few friends. Select few, of course. Some ladies, I'd imagine. Top quality drugs care of the local constabulary. More booze than you'll ever drink. Blah blah blah. You've both been to parties before, so I won't go on patronising you. You never stay for long do you Tubbs, and all the boys have been asking after you. What d'you say?"

"Why not," answered Tubbs with zero enthusiasm. He didn't want to stay the night, but knew that there was no escape either. After all, he couldn't drive.

"Fuckin'-A!" added Boda, who couldn't believe his luck. A private party in the home of a famous rock star! And to think he'd almost gone home for a wank…

As Boda and Luca bonded over the spliff, an unfamiliar figure walked absently towards them across the chippings. Tubbs hadn't seen him before but there was something oddly familiar about him as well. He was much older than the rest of the Disgraceland crew, at least twenty years, and his wild white hair formed a strange 'fro above his weathered face. He wore what can only be described as 'gardening clothes', and his hands were covered in dirt.

"Blod!" Luca welcomed him warmly, and Tubbs knew at once who he was. Disgraceland's ganja-growing guru stood before them. "Have you met Tubbs before?"

Tubbs offered his hand but the old man paused before shaking it as a strange look crossed his face. Recognition, maybe? But recognition of what Tubbs didn't know. He soon regained his composure and shook Tubbs's hand.

"And this is Boda," added Luca, but before letting go of one visitor's hand and shaking the other, Blod noticed the jade ring on Tubbs's pinky finger.

Blod couldn't believe who stood in front of him. The eyes. The mouth. The ring. There was no doubt. The chubby teenager he remembered had grown into a mountain range of a man, and the past, in the blink of an eye, had finally caught up with him. His cheeks flushed crimson but before Tubbs had the chance to ask him what was wrong, Blod hastily turned to Boda, shook his hand and walked away without another word.

"What was wrong with him?" asked Tubbs.

"Nothing," came Luca's oblivious answer. "Blod can be a bit weird at times, that's all. He's not the most social person you'll ever meet. Take no offence…"

"Ok," said Tubbs as he realised that no one else had even noticed the gardener's strange behaviour.

Luca dropped everything – not that he had a lot to do that afternoon anyway – and led the visitors to the guest wing. Along the way, he showed them a few personal favourites from his extensive art collection, which hung on the manor house's seemingly endless walls, and memorabilia from his own career and those of some of his other favourite artists, and by the time they arrived at the bedroom on the first floor, overlooking the pool, Tubbs's leg was on fire. Boda insisted he take off his trousers and lie on the bed, before tenderly applying the Preparation H to his friend's gaping wound. Then they left him where he was while Luca took Boda on a guided tour of the estate. On horseback, of course.

TASTE TEST

As HE drove through Dinas Powys, with one eye on the road and the other staring at the blonde piece pouting in the rear-view, Vexl knew that this one was going to be quite a challenge.

Blondie was quiet and pissed-off, her eyes full of fear, as she stared at the world rolling by the half-open window. No one had said anything much since the ruck that was their introduction. Vexl was coming down now – from the adrenaline and the amphetamine. He needed another hit, but he'd have to wait. He placed a fag between his crinkled lips, lit it and looked once again at his catch.

So young.

So scared.

So perfect.

Was she all out of hope, or planning her escape? The first option, Vexl hoped.

The drum, the bass and the heavy dub of the Hi-Fi Killers boomed from the car stereo, while Gimp nodded his head to the rhythm and toked hard on another Red Cherry. Vexl wound down his window to let out some smoke, his head empty all of a sudden.

The driver's words about her 'new life' had frozen Petra to the very core. She felt completely out of her depth. The valley girl with a head full of dreams now had a full-blown nightmare to contend with. She couldn't talk, or at least didn't want to, just in case she dug herself in any deeper. But despite her oral paralysis, her head was alive as it tried to find a way out.

Some facts were very clear. Number one – she was riding with a couple of very bad men. Gangsters of some kind. Criminals, without a doubt. Pimps at best. People traffickers, at the very worse. Number two – she'd been kidnapped. Quite a dramatic conclusion, maybe, but there was no denying it either. That's where the definite facts ended though. Of course, she could speculate all day about them and what they would do to her when they reached wherever they were going, but what use would that be?

As they passed Llandough Hospital, Petra reached a decision. She had to escape. Whatever they had in store for her, she had to get away from this pair at the first opportunity. To do this she'd have to be brave. But more than that, she'd have to be clever. Or cleverer than her captors at least. Firstly, she'd have to go along with whatever they had in store for her, try to earn their trust and wait for the exact moment to make her escape. Her mind raced as she thought of the possibilities – most too hideous to even consider. She shook her head to clear the mist, raised a smile, pulled back the curtains, stepped onto the stage and prepared to wow this crowd of two with a performance of Olivier Award-winning proportions.

"So, where to are we goin' then boys? It betta 'ave a kettle cos I'm fucken parched…" she said, as cool and as calm as she could.

"So," said Gimp as he turned to look at her. "You can talk as well as scream…"

"Yeah, sorry 'bout tha luv, it was a birrofa shock, that's all… I mean, it's not every day you gets kidnapped, is it?"

Vexl listened and watched as the scene unfolded in the rear-view, allowing Gimp to do the talking.

"Kidnapped!" Gimp exploded. "Steady on dahlin', I just saved ya fackin life back vere! Vat huge bastard was about to stab ya…"

"An' I'm very grateful for tha…" retorted Petra, her blue eyes glinting. She wanted to ask him what he was doing down the alley, but winding him up wouldn't help. "So where we goin' then?"

"Yah'll see," Vexl joined in, and although his voice filled her with terror, she smiled at the dread's red eyes as they stared at her in the mirror.

"Seriously now, are you gonna hurt me or wha?"

"Nah nah, nuffin like va'!" Gimp answered, slightly offended, which made Petra's answer even more unexpected.

"Oh," Petra said, her voice filled with disappointment. "That's a shame…" She left it hanging there and reached over to touch Gimp's knee, before grabbing her fags and leaning in for a light, giving him a glimpse of the wonders that bulged before her. Regardless of her external ease, on the inside she was in pieces.

Gimp fumbled with the lighter before finally managing to light her cigarette, while Vexl watched with wonder, not quite able to believe his luck. She'd gone from ice queen to slut of the year in the space of a few miles.

Before Petra finished her smoke, Vexl pulled up outside a terraced house on a shabby street. While finishing her cigarette she looked out of the window at the grottfest that bore the misleading name of Barry Island Pleasure Park. She opened the car door and stepped out to the joyous screams of the unseen patrons whizzing around the log flume, the dodgems or carousel, and she suddenly remembered visiting the fair sometime during her childhood on a daytrip with the local youth club. Back then it was all Mr Whippy's and greasy chips, sunburned skin and sandy toes, as opposed to today's visit to this house of unimaginable horrors.

She looked up and down the street, trying to remember which way they came. She recalled passing the strangely-named Safari Inn about a mile or so ago, not far from Dow Corning's smoke-spewing industrial chimneys. They passed a Maccy Ds on a roundabout near Dinas Powys, but apart from that she couldn't remember much.

Gimp led the way, while Vexl followed the new recruit. Vexl seemed quite terrifying sat down behind the wheel, but Petra was now officially petrified. Dressed all in black and standing close to six foot five, face half-hidden behind thick dreads and his eyes glowing amber, he reminded Petra of the Predator. Which was not a good thing.

Gimp filled the kettle when they reached the kitchen at the back of the house, while Vexl sat at the table silently crushing some pills using a huge hunting knife. Petra sat down and smiled at the skinny girl who walked in. She was glad that there was someone else there, even if she did look like a smacked-out skeleton.

"Vicky, vis is Petra, our new girl. Petra, vis is Vicky, our old girl," Vicky smiled, sadly.

Petra smiled back and knew at once that this place was a brothel and that Vicky was a whore. This probably made her one too, at least for the time being.

"So what now, when do I get started?" asked Petra, serving herself on a platter. On hearing this, Vexl almost blew the powder he was about to hoover up his snout off the table.

"We'll have a cuppa first and ven get dahn to business, is it Vex?"

"Yah mon," answered the boss, before caning the chemicals and closing his eyes to ride the initial rush. "Den we gyet dyahn ta biznuz."

The tea disappeared in a whirlwind of abuse. Petra watched as Vexl and Gimp each snorted a couple of lines off the kitchen table, while Vicky swallowed three blue pills that Vexl handed her. She'd been around drugs and drug-takers plenty of times in the past, but this was different somehow. This was serious business, with little or no fun involved. And when Vexl wrapped a huge joint which was shared between them along with a second cup of tea, Petra's head swam around the kitchen on the back of a unicorn, leaving her decapitated body sitting in silence, hoping that no one would notice. During her trance, Petra had what can only be described as a moment of clarity, and once again she realised the seriousness of the situation she now found herself in. So when she came to once more, she finished her cuppa and set the ball rolling because the sooner they got on with it the sooner she could try getting out of here.

"Ready!" she exclaimed, getting up from the table.

"Fackin 'ell, steady on dahlin!" Gimp had never met such an enthusiastic new girl as Petra. She was pretty special, he could see that now.

"Nah mon, tha's cool." Vexl appreciated her willingness, which made his life much simpler…

"You want me to show her the room?" Vicky offered.

"Nah yet. Yah wanna show wha yah cyan do?"

"You wanna see me dance, is tha it?"

"Nah quite," Vexl laughed at her naivety, before his glee subsided. "I wanna see yah fuck da Gimpmon. Yah cyan cyall it a taste test…"

"No way!" Vicky cried. "Don't do it Vex, please!" She pleaded, looking from Vexl to Gimp and back again. Vexl ignored her, stared at Petra to see how she would react; while Gimp shrugged his shoulders in a weak gesture that said 'I'm sorry, luv, but what can I do', while simultaneously loosening his belt.

Vicky got up and left the kitchen. She stormed upstairs, stormed back down a few seconds later, then stormed out the front door, swearing and muttering in their general direction.

Internally, Petra was shitting it. But externally, she smiled, looked at Gimp, licked her lips and purred.

"Mmmmmm, I was 'oping you'd say tha," she stepped

towards him. "Come ere little man, let's see what you've got down there…" but Petra wasn't quite prepared for the beast that burst from his boxers. Not that it was big. It was *huge*. By far the biggest cock she'd ever seen. In real life. Maybe Gimp was a small man in terms of his stature, but he was a giant in this specific department.

After swallowing her surprise, Petra headed for the lounge. "Put a johnny on and follow me," she barked as she went, before trying her best to switch off all emotions, every feeling, and detach herself from her own mind and body. In many ways doing so was quite similar to meditation, or an out-of-body experience and Petra had practiced the art in the period of time since she started selling tricks almost three years ago. By now she could switch off to such an extent that it was almost as if these acts happened to someone else. Almost.

With both hoods in tow – one eager and almost fully erect, the other well-impressed but flaccid – Petra lifted her skirt and peeled down her thong, placed her hands on the arm of the surprisingly smart leather sofa, inviting the little man to enter. Gimp's cock stiffened and he thanked a god which he didn't believe in for his good fortune. What a job! He stepped to her, peeling the rubber over his shaft and spitting on his bell to ease the entry.

Vexl sat in the comfy chair on the other side of the lounge, under a framed print of Edvard Munch's most famous painting. He sparked another chunky joint, although it didn't come close to the girth of Gimp's cock.

"What you waiten for?" asked Petra, as she watched Gimp through heavily glazed eyes shuffle towards her like a garden gnome pushing a purple wheelbarrow. When she left Merthyr this morning, she hadn't expected things to turn out quite like this, but she knew what she had to do to escape and this, unfortunately, was part of the plan. "C'mon big man, fuck me now," said a voice that she barely recognised – her subconscious had taken over.

Gimp didn't need a second invitation and with the thick green spittle acting like lube, he stepped onto a low leather pouffe and entered her very carefully. Of course, he was fully aware of the pain his penis could cause, as he'd made many a girl weep by merely part-penetrating them. He didn't want to hurt Petra though, as she'd hopefully be making him and Vexl some money before the end of the day. Tomorrow at the latest.

By the time Gimp's super-tanker was fully docked in her harbour, Petra was completely detached from this world. She was floating deep within the pleasure palace that was her imagination. Her body was still there, of course, but her soul was somewhere else entirely.

She found herself standing on a bridge in a beautiful garden – a fragrant Eden bursting with life, both floral and faunal. Flowers and plants surrounded her, birds chirped in the trees above, sparkling silver fish swam in the stream below. There were cats everywhere. And guarding the glass-domed palace at the end of the winding path, she saw a silent and gentle giant, who watched as Petra crouched down to stroke one of the feline residents who'd come for a closer look. Petra looked up and saw the giant staring directly at her. She smiled. He looked away, unsure how he should react. Petra stood and walked towards him, but he disappeared into the undergrowth before she got near. She followed once more, and this time he came to meet her. He took her in his arms, whispered in her ear. She felt safe here and that's where she stayed for the rest of the day – with the colossus and the cats – as her body was abused back on planet earth…

She passed her test with an A* and spent the rest of the day in her new bedroom, waiting for an opportunity to escape while servicing a few clients. Unfortunately, although she was pretty sure that she'd convinced Vexl with her act, he didn't trust her yet and neither he nor Gimp left the house during the rest of the day. She'd have to be patient, she concluded, as 'Walter', her fourth customer who reeked of Fisherman's Friends and rising damp, shot his load over her tits while apologising and muttering something about his mother under his breath, before leaving the room with tears streaming down his cheeks...

Watching Gimp giving it to the new girl in the front room, the phet rushing round his bloodstream and a hefty scoob burning away between his thumb and forefinger, the scene reminded Vexl of a Yorkshire terrier fucking an Afghan hound. Not that he'd ever seen such a thing, of course. *Cyan it gyet any worse dan dis, mon?* he asked himself as his friend grunted and gargled his way to climax. A sinister, dark voice echoed somewhere deep within him, followed by some unexplainable feeling that this was only the beginning. But of what, he didn't know. *Storms ah brewin, Vexmon.*

"E'nuff!" he growled, when it all became too much. The girl was *uh*-ing and *ah*-ing and generally putting on a bit of a show, but her eyes were glazed and distant. Almost dead.

"No way Vex, I'm not even close to shootin' my load!" Gimp grunted, as he continued to thrust.

"Gerroff 'er, Gimpmon, NOW!" And just like that, Gimp extracted the beast and ran to the bog to empty his sacks with an inadequate posh-wank, cursing Vexl with every stroke.

Vexl sent Petra to her room, told her to take a shower and gave her a pack of super slims and a bag of grass. Nothing too strong, just enough to take the edge off.

"Yah dun good, girly. Nah go watch samh tee-vee, get stoned, wait fah yah firs' customah," and off she went like a good girl, eyes as vacant as a disused shop. Vexl couldn't quite believe his luck, so he grabbed a couple of pills from his pocket and started crushing them on the coffee table, just in time for Gimp's return.

Vicky returned to the house and quietly opened the door. She felt a little better after a walk on the beach. While watching the waves do their thing she realised that she had no right to be fucked off with Gimp for what he did. Except maybe his enthusiasm. But she couldn't even blame him for that really. After all, he was as enslaved as she was to Vexl, their dark lord and master.

She could hear voices coming from the lounge, so she leaned in a little closer.

"She's summin' else, vis one Vex." Vicky was gutted – it was Gimp's helium-high voice.

"Tru mon, she be headin to Kiadiff in nah time."

"I reckon. I fought she'd be a fackin nightmare when we picked er up, vough."

"Too tru. She soon ciam rahnd mon!" And then the bastards laughed and congratulated each other on a good day's work.

Vicky heard Vexl hoover a line off the coffee table, so she went upstairs, via the kitchen, to have a word with the new recruit.

From the drawer by the sink, she grabbed a bread knife – the sharpest one they had – before heading to blondie's bedroom. But when she got there, the door was closed and some punter was laying his pipe, so she headed for her own pad to wait for him to leave.

Petra wasn't the only one who'd have to be patient today…

By ten o'clock that night, Petra had sucked four cocks of varying flaccidity, been rogered twice (not including Gimp), had her tits splattered by one poor soul's semen and yawned her way through an extremely repetitive hand job that came close to giving her carpal tunnel syndrome.

After a long shower – the fourth of the day – she sat on her bed in her underwear, sucking on a nice strong spliff, blowing the smoke towards the open window and encouraging the room's other bad smells to follow suit. Gimp came up after the last customer had left and told her she wouldn't have to work any more tonight. Thank fuck. Vexl was 'well impressed' according to the vertically challenged Manaconda. He took the money and praised her attitude, which suggested that her act was working, before leaving her to it.

Through glazed eyes, she watched the lights of the nearby funfair flicker and listened to the voices of those lucky enough to be free, screaming with delight as the log flume once again crashed into the water from ten feet. She considered trying to squeeze out the tiny window and do a runner right away, but knew that she'd never make it.

She lay back against the headboard and reached for her book in an attempt to escape from reality for a little while. But, before reading a single word the door swung open and there stood Vicky. In her hand she carried a huge knife. In her eyes, pure hatred.

"Alright, Vic?" Petra asked, instinctively getting up and staring at the sorry sight that was standing on the other side of the bed.

"You-can't-go-they-all-go-except-I-stay…" Vicky spat, rat-a-tat-tat.

"What? Where d'they go, luv, what you on about?"

"You-all-leaves-me-you-do. You-all-leaves-like…"

"Slow down, slow down and for fuck's sake drop the knife!"

"You-gotta-stay-with-me. Don't-go…"

"I'm not goin' nowhere, luv, onest now…" How the fuck

did this one know of her plan? Petra wondered, before Vicky revealed the truth as well as her intention.

Petra held her book tightly in her right hand. She could deal with Vicky if she had to – after all, she was in far better shape and towered above her, even in her socks.

Vicky shuffled around the foot of the bed before suddenly lunging towards Petra, knife aimed at that pretty face, just like she'd seen Vexl do so many times over the years, but Petra was too quick and managed to avoid the strike by jumping on to the bed and over to the other side. Vicky turned at once and dived after her but once again Petra side-stepped with ease while Vicky lost her footing and found herself on the floor, eating carpet and staring at her quarry's toes.

Petra watched as Vicky struggled to her feet. She didn't feel any animosity towards her. Just pity, for she was well and truly fucking pathetic. Hands on knees, Vicky panted, so Petra leaned in to console her and that's when she pounced. Up came the knife, missing Petra's face by a matter of millimetres, and this time she made her pay. For the second time that day, Petra used her book as a tennis racket, back-handing Vicky hard across her cheek, making the blood from her nose burst and spray onto the faded anaglypta. With Vicky crumpled in a heap on the floor, Petra grabbed the knife, set it aside and dragged her attacker out the room by her hair before closing the door and locking it behind her.

BAD CALL

W ITH THE sight of Calvin's headless corpse flashing before Foxy's eyes each time she blinked, the sound of her and Little Al's footsteps echoing off the walls of the vast empty foyer at Cardiff Central train station did nothing but enhance her ever-growing paranoia. By now, Foxy had convinced herself that the police were on their trail, and her eyes were open wide and full to the brim with fear as she ushered her young son towards the exit and the dark city that awaited them beyond.

She was relieved that there were no coppers anywhere to be seen. In fact, except for the handful of passengers that left the same train as them, and the trio of tramps snoring under their inadequate bed covers made of old potato sacks, the whole place was deserted, which suited her just fine.

Foxy's pulse eased a little as soon as they stepped out into the night. She was glad that Al seemed oblivious to the drama. Directly in front of them stood the dark and dormant bus station. To the left, the Empire Pool and the River Taf. To the right, the Central Hotel – their destination.

"You ok, luv?"

"Yes," Little Al yawned, so Foxy took his hand and led him towards their uncertain future.

The streets were almost as quiet as the station itself, and apart from two taxis and a cluster of bikers parked outside the Wimpy Bar sharing a bottle of Jack, they were alone.

"C'mon, Al," Foxy bleated when her son stopped to stare at the hairy bikers. "We're not far now, look, there's our hotel," but Little Al wouldn't move, for he was well and truly mesmerised.

Some hundred yards from the hotel, Foxy panicked when she saw the flashing lights of a police car some fifty feet in front of them on the corner of St Mary Street. Hastily – her head full of horrors – she pulled Al with her and ducked down a nearby alley to hide for a while until the police moved on. Behind some industrial bins, Foxy leaned her back against the cold wall, while Al sat on his bag and waited for his mother to sort herself out.

If only she had stopped to consider her actions for a split-second, she would have realised the foolishness of her plan, but she was acting on impulse as her common sense was being choked by trepidation. Her heartbeat thumped between her ears, her head filled with distortion and fear. She closed her eyes and massaged her temples, to no avail. Al started poking her, softly to begin with, then with increasing urgency. She opened her eyes, expecting to see a policeman standing in front of her, but what she saw was far worse.

Two men towered above them – white eyes glistening from the black canvasses of their faces. Foxy strained to see them more clearly, but it was an impossible task in the almost pitch darkness of the back alley, down behind the bins. What she could see was that one of them carried a hunting knife, while the other's weapon of choice was a crowbar. Foxy's hand inched its way into her handbag, in search of the gun, while Al stared at the bandits through eyes that had already seen much worse.

Without any warning, the one with the knife grabbed Little Al and dragged him to his feet, before turning him around and holding the blade to his windpipe.

"Your bag," the other whispered through gritted teeth, but by now Foxy's hand was gripping the Magnum. Time stood still for a few seconds. Nobody moved. Foxy looked from one attacker to the other, before settling on the face of her only son.

"Your bag!" repeated the same man, this time raising his voice slightly while lifting the crowbar over his head, but before he could bring it crashing down on Foxy's crown, she pulled the gun from her bag and pointed it straight at his cock and balls.

"A Mexican stand-off, I believe," Foxy said, standing up and swapping her target – the gun now pointed directly at the centre of Mr Crowbar's face. "Let him go and walk away slowly or I'll blow your head off," she added, with absolute authority. And although her voice might have sounded calm to her assailants, her insides were positively quaking.

With her handbag hanging over her left shoulder, she kept the gun aimed at the centre of her attacker's face. She repeated her threat just as a blinding light and a deafening rumble filled the alley. In the confusion, the one with the knife pushed Al towards her, while the other grabbed Foxy's handbag, ripping the handle and tearing it from her grasp. By the time she regained her balance, they were gone.

As the motorbike slowly rumbled nearer, Foxy crouched down and held her son tightly. An awful evening had just turned into a terrible night. As the truth sank in, Foxy started cursing and muttering like a mental patient. What could they do now? The money would have set them up nicely, allowed them to make a new start…

The light dipped and the engine stopped growling. Foxy heard heavy footsteps approaching, echoing off the walls of the narrow alley, followed by a smoky voice enquiring.

"What's going on? You two ok?"

Foxy looked up at the latest stranger to cross their path, tears streaming silently down her cheeks. He was one of the bikers from outside the Wimpy; the only one who stood out from the rest of the crowd of walking talking clichés. And the reason for that was his silver mane and similarly coloured handlebar moustache. Comfortably middle-aged, he was very handsome and possessed the physique of a man twenty years his junior. He smiled at Foxy, but she couldn't return the greeting. She was livid and wanted to hurt this man for the part he played in their misfortune. She had the situation under control, until *he* came along. She raised the gun, stood up and walked slowly towards him.

"You fuckin' dick!" She spat, as the biker lifted his hands in submission, stepping backwards as she narrowed the gap. "What the fuck is wrong with you?"

"Whoa, whoa!" He pleaded, his back against the wall, the gun pointing right up his nose. "Put the gun down, luv, before you hurt someone."

In the blink of an eye, Foxy moved the gun to the left of the stranger's head and fired a shot that exploded off the brickwork, deafening all three of them and echoing forever in the dark.

"Jesus fuckin' Christ!" The stranger exclaimed, covering his ears with his hands. He saw the fear in her eyes; the hopelessness in her heart. She started pounding his chest with the butt of the gun and her other closed fist. The tears gushed and the expletives too. He heard money mentioned, but the details were drowned out by the wailing. He let her hit him until she weakened, then grabbed her by the wrists and pulled her to him.

"You ok, little man?" he asked the boy over his mother's still-shuddering shoulder.

Al nodded his answer, although he wasn't certain that he was.

"Where you heading?" he turned his attention back to Foxy, who was still all of a sudden, as if the drama had drained all of her strength.

"We *were* heading to the Central Hotel," she whispered. "But all our money was in my handbag, which was just stolen, thanks to *you*…" Foxy started hitting him once again, but before the stranger had a chance to sort the situation, the alley was once again flooded with light and the rumblings of an engine.

The biker grabbed her arms and pulled the one that held the gun out of sight, down to her side. "Tuck the piece down the back of your knickers and let me do the talking," he whispered, before adding: "Do it quick. We haven't got time to discuss it," when he saw Foxy was about to argue. "It's the cops, so unless you want to spend the night in the cells explaining where you got your hands on that gun, do as I say,"

She slipped the steel between her waistband and bare back while the biker shielded her movements from the approaching filth. The car stopped some ten yards short of the scene, and both officers stepped out of the vehicle although they didn't approach. They left the lights on, so that their subjects had to use their hands to protect their eyes.

"Is there a problem here?"

"Not at all, officer," the biker answered, his smile almost filling the alley. "The missus is a bit upset cos I was late picking her and the boy up from the train, that's all." He gestured towards the baggage, as if that answered everything.

"I wasn't asking *you*, sir," came the reply. "Miss, is everything alright here?"

Foxy nodded. Smiled weakly. "Yes, officer."

"We heard a…"

"That was my bike," answered the biker, butting in. "Needs a service, keeps backfiring. We'll be off in a minute now, as soon as we get these bags loaded…"

If this encounter had taken place at the start of their shift, as opposed to half an hour from the end of it, they probably would have pursued the matter a little further. Instead, the police officers looked dubiously at the three of them, before climbing back into their car and slowly reversing up the alley the way they came, due to the fact that the motorbike was blocking their path.

"What now?" asked Foxy, as she watched them park up at the mouth of the alley.

"Well, I guess you haven't got much choice really. As you can see, those two are keeping an eye on us to see what we do next," he nodded towards the patrol car. "So, unless you want to have another chat with them, maybe explain to them why you're carrying a big gun with you, we should grab your things and go back to my place. What do you reckon, little man – fancy a ride on my chopper?"

Little Al, his ears still ringing, smiled his reply and reached for his bag. He hoped he'd never see another gun in his life after tonight, but was more than happy to take the biker up on his offer. Foxy on the other hand, didn't like this one bit, but she reluctantly did as the stranger suggested, because the last thing she wanted was another run-in with the law. While gathering her belongings from the floor, Foxy looked up to see Calvin's still warm, headless cadaver leaning casually on a wheelie bin by her side, pouring whisky directly down his neck. She shook her head, which made the apparition disappear, and soon found herself riding pillion – with Al sandwiched between her and T-Bone, their luggage strapped to the back of the hog using some rope – along the quiet city streets, out of the centre of town towards the suburbs and beyond.

Foxy had the shock of her life when they reached their destination as she fully expected T-Bone's home to be located above a garage somewhere, full to the brim with mechanic's tools and Black Sabbath records, as opposed to the rural manor house in Rudry that was his actual residence. However, as shocked as she was, it must also be noted that she was more than pleased with this outcome.

As the few days became a few weeks, T-Bone's love for Foxy bloomed, while the initial spark she felt towards him soon dampened and died a quick death.

At the beginning of their 'relationship', T-Bone overwhelmed Foxy with gifts of love – from the ridiculous in the form of a pink chopper, 'hers' to 'his' manly hog (which she traded in for a Mini before even attempting to ride it); to the extreme in the form of a timber house in Dinas Powys, located on the other side of the city; which was supposed to give Foxy a degree of independence, while in reality it did nothing other than ensuring that she was indebted to him forever.

Furthermore, T-Bone and Al became best friends within minutes of meeting. Not only did their relationship help Al come out of his shell, but it also helped him bury what he had done to Calvin mere hours before their initial encounter. In Foxy's eyes, both of these things were to be welcomed, especially the fact that Al suddenly had a positive male role model in his life. However, the downside to this was that the more Al and T-Bone bonded, the harder it was for her to ever leave…

T-Bone took full advantage of Foxy's lack of funds and bleak prospects and imprisoned her psychologically like some post-modern Petrosinella. Due to the fact that he'd 'saved' her from a hard life servicing the desperate men of Wales' second city, T-Bone felt a sense of ownership over Foxy, just like Calvin before him. And although she moved to Dinas Powys in an attempt to put some distance between them, her job working behind the bar at the Bandidos' clubhouse and Little Al's eagerness to spend every waking minute with his new hero, meant that she spent most of her time at T-Bone's home anyway.

The main problem was T-Bone's nature. He was a jealous bastard who, despite his age, often acted like an infant. And as the respected leader of a successful and violent organised crime syndicate, he expected everyone to obey his every command, while he also tried to control anyone he came into contact with. Furthermore, he was lonely and had never tasted true love, until Foxy came along. Unfortunately for all concerned, that love wasn't reciprocated.

The months turned into years and the adults' relationship had long reached a barren plateau of half-forced friendship. However, their relationship wasn't a complete vacuum either, mainly due to the fact that T-Bone loved Foxy almost unconditionally, while his connection with Little Al still grew stronger by the day, based mainly on a shared love of motorbikes and air rifles. Foxy felt like some kind of trophy, especially when she was given special attention when working behind the bar at the clubhouse or when T-Bone was entertaining guests or business associates. The whole thing was a farce, as they both lay like a couple of felled trees next to each other at night, when Foxy would stay over at the mansion.

Increasingly, when she did stay, Foxy would lie in the dark staring into oblivion, weighing up her options, while T-Bone snored like a boar beside her. And although she longed to bring the 'relationship' to an end, she could see, could sense, that wasn't even an option. She was as imprisoned today as she was in Calvin's clutches. She longed for something better, but unlike the fairytales that her life seemed to mirror, she knew that even if a prince *would* come and rescue her from her metaphorical tower, they'd both be hunted down by the evil king and his hog-riding hordes, before being killed and cooked in a boiling cauldron. On a more practical note, she also knew that if she left T-Bone she'd lose her home in the Vale and the security and sanctuary of being 'with' the leader of the Bandidos, while also risking losing her only son, who these days was closer to T-Bone than he was to her.

And that's if she actually escaped with her life. She didn't even want to start imagining what T-Bone would do to her if she tried to leave. She'd seen enough over the years and heard plenty of rumours to know that T-Bone was a sadistic and merciless man, who would never stand for such disrespect.

Although Foxy had never been unfaithful to T-Bone during their time together, and regardless of the obvious threat to her wellbeing if she did anything to betray him, everything changed on Little Al's seventeenth birthday.

The date was 4 June 1987, and Foxy lay by the pool enjoying the peace and quiet, not to mention the brilliant sunshine, wearing a tiny silver bikini which sparkled and gleamed and generally showed off her body to anyone who cared to look her way.

Little Al and T-Bone had disappeared for the day as they went out for Al's first legal bike ride, on the brand new chopper that T-Bone had bought him for his birthday. Aberystwyth was mentioned, but that seemed a heck of a long way to go for a ride, but then these bikers were a right bunch of nutters, she knew that all too well.

Her back and bum-cheeks started to burn, so she turned around slowly on her sunbed in order to bronze her belly and her boobs, and as she did so, she noticed the gardener hard at work on the other side of the pool. He was almost naked, except for a pair of tiny, tight, cut-up denim shorts and the well-worn work boots on his feet. She watched him from behind her sunglasses as he stopped whatever he was doing and stood up to take a long sip of water from a bottle he had close to hand. His mane of wild hair reminded her of a lion, and she felt her lips quiver involuntarily, moistening beneath her bikini.

The sweat glistened on his tightly-muscled torso, and Foxy could practically taste the salty fluid from the other side of the pool. She licked her lips and couldn't avert her gaze, even if she wanted to. She hadn't felt like this for years. In fact, she couldn't remember *ever* wanting anyone as much as she wanted the gardener right this very second.

And as if he could read her mind, he placed the bottle down on the ground and walked slowly towards her. Foxy's heart started beating like a bongo. His body was perfectly sculpted. Not *too* muscly. Just nice and toned. She tried guessing his age, but he could be anything between twenty-five and forty. His face was well-weathered and he had a smile that instantly melted the iceberg that was her long-neglected heart.

He kneeled at the bottom of Foxy's sunbed, seemingly contemplating his opening line.

"D'you wanna see my cactus?" he asked eventually with a cheeky grin, taking Foxy fully by surprise.

She returned his smile, but had a question of her own.

"You *do* know who I am, don't you?"

"Of course. The boss's wife…"

"Wrong!" exploded Foxy, holding her left hand in front of her.

"Well, excuse me, madam!" came the over-courteous reply. "Please accept my apology for being so ignorant."

"You're forgiven," Foxy said, giggling like a schoolgirl.

"But you *do* live here. *With* the boss."

"Yes. On and off. But how do you know so much about me?" The game was only just beginning, but Foxy had already fallen for his charm.

"D'you promise not to tell anyone?"

Foxy nodded.

"Ok. Well, I've been watching you since the first day I started working here…"

"Really?" Foxy purred, sitting up and leaning closer. "Anything else to confess?"

"Yes. I've never seen anyone quite like you in my whole life," came the reply, without any hesitation. "Now, what about my cacti? I'm going to water them now, if you want to give me a hand…" And with that, he stood up and walked away, leaving Foxy lying by the pool, staring at his buns and weighing up her options.

Before turning the corner and heading for the greenhouses, he looked over his shoulder at Foxy once again, silently urging her to follow. Still she sat. Had he misjudged the situation? And just as he thought she wouldn't budge, she got to her feet and followed.

He turned the corner and disappeared from view, but when Foxy reached the first greenhouse, where the gardener grew his tomatoes, he was waiting for her, leaning against the doorframe.

"I'm Andrew, by the way, but everyone calls me Blod," he said as he drew her near and held her for the first time.

"Well, I'm gonna call you Andrew. Ok?"

"Whatever you wish. You're Foxy, right?"

"But you can call me Lisa…"

"Ok, *Lisa*, I have a small confession."

"What?"

"I haven't got any cacti…"

During the following year, Foxy and Blod spent as much time as was secretively possible in each other's company. He made her feel so free, although in reality she was more restricted than ever due to their relationship. But she didn't care: he put a smile on her face and filled her heart with joy – something no one had ever managed before. Fortunately, T-Bone was almost fully focused on his business affairs. And when his time wasn't taken up by various dodgy ventures, he lavished Al with attention. The pair had grown ever closer since Little Al had officially reached adulthood, and Foxy found herself spending more and more time at her home in Dinas Powys, which helped her and Blod's love deepen even further. Of course, T-Bone knew that his relationship with Foxy was floundering, but he chose to go the way of the ostrich, and buried his head in the sand while his asshole struggled to keep watch.

Blod built three greenhouses in her beautifully unkempt garden: one to grow tomatoes; one for grapes, strawberries and cape gooseberries; and the other to house his own special crop – a dark and funky strain of Jamaican collieweed. During this happy period, and with Andrew by her side, Foxy learnt how to be a gardener. In fact, her interest soon bloomed to be a full-blown passion.

The lovers lived in a bubble of calm sunshine, surrounded by dark and threatening thunder clouds. They had four cats, including a kitten named Victor that Blod gave her as a gift to celebrate their six month 'anniversary'. Regardless of the ever-widening divide between herself and T-Bone, Foxy was never quite able to escape his looming shadow. As Blod's boss and her keeper, the head-Bandido had an unrelenting influence over their lives.

And what's more, Foxy missed her son so much that when he asked if he could move to Dinas Powys for a few weeks to spend some time with her about a year after Blod and her first met, she agreed without hesitation and in the space of one phone call, the lovers' privacy and freedom was abruptly ended.

The following day Foxy headed to Rudry in her blood red Mini Cooper, for a spot of lunch and to collect Little Al's bags as he couldn't carry everything he wished to bring on the back of his bike.

On her arrival, T-Bone squeezed her tight and nuzzled her neck as the gravel crunched underfoot.

"Mmmmmmm, when you gonna stay the night next, Foxy? I miss you, babe."

"Well, not until after Al's hols…" came the answer, as she broke free of his grasp and headed up the stone steps towards the house.

She still slept with T-Bone – physically, but not emotionally – from time to time, at least once a fortnight, just to keep him sweet and off the scent. Blod was aware of the arrangement and conceded that this was the only way for them to maintain their relationship without drawing T-Bone's unwanted attention.

Little Al, who was now a full-grown man sporting an untidy beard, stood at the door, smiling broadly at his mother. Foxy walked right up to him and playfully pinched his still-chubby cheeks.

"Hiya, babe, d'you miss your little old mam then, or what? And here I was thinking you and T-Bone were having loads of fun without me."

"He's not the only one," T-Bone retorted, as Al swatted his mother away before giving her a huge bear hug.

They ate a tasty lunch outside on the patio, next to the shimmering pool, and appeared to the whole world as a pretty normal family. After finishing, Al went up to his room to collect his things, leaving his mam to deal with T-Bone, who was like a hound harassing a bitch in heat this afternoon. As T-Bone's hands wandered up her leg with some purpose, she thought of Andrew and suddenly remembered that due to Al's visit, they needed to change their plan for the following evening, so she got up and walked away, leaving T-Bone with a raging horn and no way of relieving the rigidity.

"I've got to pee, luv," Foxy said as she left the table.

"Really? Ok, luv. But don't be long…" answered T-Bone, as he readjusted his boner and took a swig of beer. Bottle in hand, he sat there contemplating life for a minute, and came to the conclusion that this would be his last chance to get any action for at least a fortnight, if not longer, so he got up and followed her to the bog. He walked through the kitchen and could see at once that the toilet door, on the other side of the huge hallway, was wide open, which was a little strange as Foxy always insisted on closing it whenever nature called.

T-Bone headed for the toilet, just to make sure she wasn't in there, before standing completely still outside the empty lavatory. With his eyes closed he listened intently, allowing his ears to search the vicinity. He could hear Foxy's voice whispering close by and after slipping off his boots he stealthily followed the murmur to its source, behind the partly-closed door of his office, located off the hall next to the house's grand entrance. He stood outside and listened – intrigued on the one hand, and already angry on the other. What he heard didn't help matters either. In fact, what Foxy had to say to whoever was on the other end of the line broke his heart and blew his mind.

"I gotta be quick, alright luv. Change of plan for tomorrow night…" Foxy regretted making the call even before Blod answered. She should never take such risks, especially not in T-Bone's house.

"Why?"

"Because of Al. He'll be staying at my house for a while…"

"Oh yes. I hadn't forgotten. Honest."

"Yeah, yeah. Anyway, we should meet in a hotel or something. Somewhere neutral. Somewhere *naughty*. Can you think of anywhere?"

"I can as it happens. The Safari Inn, Holton Road, Barry," answered Blod as he recalled a discussion he had earlier that morning with a couple of co-workers about a very similar subject.

"That's sorted then. Seven o'clock. Safari Inn. Tomorrow night. Can you book a room under Mr and Mrs Jones? I don't think I'll have a chance…"

"Of course. No problemo. I've got you a surprise as well…"

"Wwww! Promises, promises. I'll see you tomorrow. I've gotta go…" She replaced the receiver and breathed deeply. Her hands were shaking. What was she thinking? Why didn't she wait? Fuck it, she'd only been gone a few seconds…

After regaining her composure, Foxy left the office and headed back the way she came – across the hall, through the kitchen and out onto the patio, where she found T-Bone and Al sitting by the table, deep in conversation and totally oblivious to her little misdemeanour.

"You ready, Mam?" asked Al, standing up and grabbing hold of his bags. "I'll chuck these in your boot and follow you on my chopper. I'm not one hundred percent sure of the way like."

"Well that just shows how often you come and see me, doesn't it?" She replied with a cheeky smile.

Past the pool and down the steps they went; a seemingly happy family. But, as T-Bone watched them leave, his thoughts ran wild, his heart lay shattered in its cage and Foxy's words echoed infinitely between his ears: *Safari Inn, tomorrow night, seven o'clock. Safari Inn, tomorrow night, seven o'clock. Safari Inn, tomorrow night, seven o'clock. Safari Inn, tomorrow night, seven o'clock…*

THE TRUTH HURTS

"Alright then, a grand. F-f-f-f-inal offer," Pennar dribbled in the direction of Maya, Milla, Mia or whatever her name was, and regretted not ensuring the presence of at least a handful of pros at tonight's party. With the time ticking towards ten o'clock, he was as well-oiled as a tin of tuna.

In front of him, slightly leathered and standing on a pair of shaky, yet shapely, legs, was an absolute peach. She leaned her manicured hands on the bar in Disgraceland's billiard room, closed her eyes slowly and contemplated the offer.

By her side stood Boda, not quite believing his luck. With a self-served quadruple JD on the rocks in one hand, his other held a credit card which he used to crush the mound of magic dust that lay before him on the bar, which he'd been given earlier in the evening by Luca as a gift, with the direct order to get 'off his tits'.

Around them, the party was properly pumping as everyone present enjoyed Luca's hospitality. The memorably-monikered Garden of Edam DJs had been spinning some classics for the best part of two hours from their base out by the pool, and the dancefloor was already heaving with honeys, while the men looked on through beet-red eyes.

"A grand? Why, what's *wrong* with him?" asked the girl in an accent rooted somewhere on the other side of Offa's Dyke. She was the fourth girl they'd approached in the space of an hour, as their mission to get Tubbs laid proved far more difficult than they'd ever imagined. Once again, this one was dubious, although the cash almost had her hooked, Pennar could sense that when she paused.

"He's a bit oversensitive, that's all," Boda joined in the

discussion just as he finished racking-up a trio of chunky lines. He took one huge toke on the joint that came his way before passing it on to the girl in the hope that it would cloud her mind and seal the deal.

"Is *that* all – a bit of a mummy's boy, is he?" she asked, before hitting the spliff and holding the smoke in her lungs for an eternity. Boda and Pennar looked at each other in response to the accuracy of her presumption, but didn't say a word. "What's the catch then – is he deformed or summin'?"

"Not at all. In fact he's a bit of an Adonis if truth be told…"

"He's ripped to the tits…"

"What d'you mean, he's off his face on summin?"

"No, no, nothing like that. In fact, he's probably the only sober cunt here tonight. What I mean is he's well built, stacked, you know, muscles everywhere. And I should know – I'm his tattooist…"

"Mmmmm, I love tats!"

"Well, you'll love the big man then, cos he's covered in 'em…"

"If there's no catch, why are you two trying to buy him a shag?"

"Uhm… He finds it difficult to meet nice ladies. He's shy. No confidence. He's had his heart broken once too many…" Pennar took over again, as Boda was too busy honking snow to answer the question.

"He's so shy I don't think he's been laid this century!" Boda added, a little unnecessarily, as he came up for air, the chemicals careering around his body, rollercoasting through his veins and screaming at the white-celled ghosts. He fell silent, shivered for a few seconds, then returned to normal. Whatever that meant tonight. Then he passed the girl the tenner, and took the spliff in exchange.

"Fill your nose, dollface, this stuff'll get you in the mood for love…"

"Why, what is it?"

"Crushed rhino horn, ancient aphrodisiac…"

"What?"

"Only jokin! It's MDMA." And down she went with no further questions. Like Boda, she shivered following the initial rush as the powder took its hold, and that's when Pennar snatched the money so he could also join in the fun. Within minutes, all three of them were swaying and stuttering and hanging onto the bar for dear life, so to take the edge off a little, Boda struggled to wrap a quick one as Pennar made a right meal of fixing more drinks, before they returned to the hot topic.

"I appreciate the offer, boys, and the money's *very* tempting but I'm sort of saving myself for Luca tonight…"

"*Really*? Well well, what a surprise…" but the girl was too out of it to notice Boda's sarcasm.

"Look," started Pennar, before forgetting what he was going to say, and then remembering once again a few seconds later. "You came here in the hope of fucking Luca, right, like most, if not *all* the other girls you see swanning around the place like walking fuck-me sandwich boards. But let's face it, he can't shag you all, can he? And unfortunately for you and the other ninety-eight per cent present, Signor Parenti's already paired off for the night with some supermodel from Bilbao…"

"*Bitch*!"

"Indeed. So, the way I see it, you may as well cash in by here with us, do what you came here to do and get handsomely rewarded in the process. What d'you reckon?"

"Good plan…"

"Yeah, thanks for that Boda, but I wasn't asking you!"

"Sorry boss, lost track of things there for a sec…"

But if Boda was slightly confused, the girl was almost

convinced. Pound signs flashed before her eyes, sweeping her morals – if she actually had any in the first place – under the thick-pile carpet of doubt.

"And there's *definitely* nothing wrong with him?"

"Apart from his oversensitivity."

"Apart from *that*?"

"Absolutely nothing."

"Ok," she agreed, before sealing the deal with her own offer. "Make it two gees and I'll fuck all three of you!"

The knock on the door dragged Tubbs back from the depths of his dreams to the here and now. He sprang to attention on the king-size bed as his mind struggled to catch up. He quickly grew accustomed to the dark, helped along by the part-open curtains and the almost-full moon way beyond the double glazing.

Where am I? Another knock. *What time is it?* Voices. *Where's my gun?* Two men. *What's wrong with my leg?* One woman. Possibly two. He jumped to his feet just in time for his leg to remind him of the reason he was lying here in the first place. His knee was on fire, Boda's etchings felt as if they were filled with molten lava, as opposed to a little ink. Another knock. More giggles. Tubbs grabbed his coat, slipped his size fourteens into his untied shoes, opened the patio doors and slipped onto the balcony just as he heard a key being turned in the door behind him. He didn't have time to deal with his fucked-up friends tonight. In fact, there was only one person he wanted to talk to.

Outside on the balcony, Tubbs quickly stepped to the side of the French windows, his huge frame half-buried in thick ivy as the light from the room, which had just been turned on, flooded the vicinity. But just as he thought he was about to be rumbled, the curtains were drawn; his world was again cast into shadow.

He breathed deeply and surveyed the scene before him. The first-floor balcony overlooked the deep end of the pool, but twenty-five metres to his right the party was in full swing. The drum and the bass throbbed and vibrated, the voices cackled and howled. How the hell did he sleep through this hullabaloo? He looked on in wonder as a couple of girls dived naked into the floodlit water, before watching them frolic in the shallows like some dream he'd never had. Poolside was populated by a wide variety of mainly pretty people – models, musicians, criminals, at least one film star Tubbs recognised – while the purple haze that danced above them tickled his nostrils like an old, old friend.

Like a wounded war-veteran, Tubbs slowly climbed down the ivy and found himself on the periphery of the party, scanning the scene for someone who could help him. He needed directions, as he knew the person he wanted to talk to wouldn't be there tonight. He spotted Darren and headed towards him, sat under a patio heater on the other side of the pool – next to the DJ shelter – wearing nothing but a pair of yellow Speedos and busy cutting lines of powder on the table in front of him. But, instead of dolly-birds and hangers-on, this ginger-haired Tony Montana's only companion was some fat, sweaty so-and-so who – wearing nothing but a pair of brightly coloured Bermuda shorts – couldn't hide the fact that he was a copper.

As Blod listened to one of Foxy's favourite records – one that hadn't gone anywhere near his turntable since her death – he could hear the music from the party beating in the background. The record was *Harvest* by Neil Young – a classic through-and-through, and one that he fondly remembered listening to in front of an open fire at their love-shack in Dinas Powys. He would have smiled at the sweet memories, if it wasn't for the fact that he was crying.

The gardener sat in his comfy chair with the wood-burner doing what it did best in the corner of the living room. On the coffee table in front of him stood a half-empty bottle of Ardbeg, his favourite dram, and a large measure chilling on the rocks. On his lap sat an open box overflowing with memories. He stared at a photo of Foxy smiling her gap-toothed grin, which he had personally taken less than a week before she was killed.

He placed the photo on the arm of the chair before staring at the ring, which he held between the thumb and forefinger of his right hand, hypnotised by a grief that would never desert him. The tears kept on flowing: the last few minutes he spent with his soulmate were as fresh in his mind today as they were the day after he lost her forever.

When Mr Young started singing about '*The needle and the damage done*', Blod got up and switched off the stereo, before returning to his chair to await Little Al's visit, as his past, at last, returned to haunt him.

"No answer," the girl stated the obvious, following the third bout of knocking on Tubbs's bedroom door.

"Open the door then," Boda tried to whisper.

"He's probably still kippin'. Go on in and fuck his brains out," Pennar urged her on.

"The door's locked," said the girl, once again excelling in the evident.

"Fuck!" Pennar gnashed his teeth in light of this slight setback.

"I got a key," remembered Boda, rummaging around in his pocket and coming up trumps.

"Good work," Pennar patted him on his back as Boda bent down and attempted to locate the lock. But his vision was blurred, and finding the hole was an impossibility. Pennar took over and although his eyes were no clearer than Bo's, like a blind man looking for the back door, he somehow managed it.

They both stepped back and allowed the girl to enter.

Apprehensively she walked towards the bed, not sure what would be waiting for her. Nothing as it happens. The bed was empty, although even she could tell that it had recently been vacated. She switched on the bedside lamp and sat on the bed, facing the door. She felt a wonderful rush when her bare cheeks touched the silk bedcovers, so she called her admirers, who were hiding in the corridor, listening to the silence within.

Their faces popped around the doorframe almost at once but their initial disappointment that Tubbs wasn't there was quickly replaced by the absolute beauty that lay before them. The girl smiled and summoned them in with a slight nod of her head, and neither Boda nor Pennar needed any further encouragement…

"You see, Tubbs, my man, I'm Disgraceland's personal sheriff, in' that right, Dar'. Like Clint fuckin' Eastwood or fuckin' you know, wossisname, fuck, Branson, no, no, hang on, Bronson, that's it, no, fuck me, not Bronson, you know…"

"The Sheriff of Nottingham?" Darren suggested, winking at Tubbs across the table, where the hitman stood, barely able to conceal his loathing of the fat pig who sat, half-naked, before him.

"Fuck off, Dar', not the Sheriff of fuckin' Nottingham, no…"

"Well who then? Who the fuck are you talking about?" And while Carwyn racked his drug-addled mind, Darren turned to Tubbs. "Please excuse Carwyn, as you can see, he's off his fuckin' box tonight…"

"No worries," Tubbs shrugged.

"Pat Garrett! Pat fuckin' Garrett!" Carwyn bellowed, spit spraying everywhere.

"Who, Lesley's husband, is it?" Darren asked, ripping the piss in the hope of melting his friend's mind even further.

"What? *What*? What the fuck are you talking about now, Dar'? Seriously. What?"

"You know. Lesley Garrett. The opera singer. Is her husband called Pat?"

"*What*? No. Fuck off Darren, you fuckin' twat! Seriously now. What the fuck are you on about? And anyway, I know you're taking the piss – I've seen *Young Guns Two* in your DVD collection."

"Good film," Tubbs said, although he had no idea why.

"Too right it's a good film. It's a fffuckin' belter in fact. Apart from that Bon fuckin' Jovi song on the soundtrack, obviously," Carwyn stopped and silently scratched his forearms for no reason, then looked at Tubbs as if he'd just noticed him for the first time. He turned to Darren. "What the fuck was I talking about?"

"Opera."

"Opera? Was I? Jesus. This *is* good shit. I don't know the first fuckin' thing about opera…"

"And Pat Garr…" Tubbs joined in, hoping that this ridiculous conversation would soon end.

"Oh yeah, that's it. I'm Disgraceland's sheriff. Without me these boys would be fucked, I'm tellin' you. And you too, Tubbs. In fact, pretty much everyone here tonight would be fucked if I wasn't here looking after things…"

"But you'd be in more trouble than anyone, Carwyn. Or should I say DS Jenkins, to use your official title."

"What? Why? What you talking about now, Dar'?"

"Well look at you. You're off your face, there's a pile of chang in front of you and a good gram plastered to your nose and face. Your pockets are full of cash and I don't think I've ever heard anyone talking more shit than you in my entire life…"

"No, Darren. You're wrong. What you see in front of you is a master policeman at work. I'm fuckin' undercover as fuck,

Dar'. Deep *deep* undercover…" Carwyn pawed at his face in an attempt to get rid of some powder, but he only made things worse. *What a tool*, thought Tubbs. He wanted to walk away, but *had* to talk to Darren, if only this dick would stop jabbering.

"Can I gerr-anotha gram off ya, mate?" A new voice joined the conversation, grabbing Carwyn's attention and allowing Tubbs to get straight to the point.

"Where's Blod?" he asked Darren.

"At home in front of the fire. Probably. He never comes to our parties – too old, he claims…"

"But *where* is Blod, Darren – where does he live?"

"Oh, right, sorry. He lives in a log cabin in the woods. Go through the house, out the front door and down the drive some hundred yards. You'll see a little path on your left, follow it for another hundred yards or so and that's where he is…"

"Thanks," said Tubbs, turning to leave.

"You'll need a torch!" Darren shouted after him, and with that in mind Tubbs rounded the house so as to avoid contact with everyone inside and grabbed his Mini Mag and his Magnum from the car, before following Darren's directions and treading the dark path towards his destiny.

Beyond his home's timber cladding and the surrounding forest, the party continued to throb in the background like the beginning of a migraine, while inside, by the fire, Blod sat patiently, awaiting his fate. Growing bored with the boom-boom-boom, he got up and placed *Cristo Redentor* by Harvey Mandel on the turntable, but before a single note had been heard, his ears were pricked by the approaching footsteps. His whole body tightened as he half-expected the Grim Reaper himself to walk through the wall and appear before him, but instead, there came a knock on the door.

He gulped some whisky, steadied his nerves. Why was he being so paranoid? So what if Little Al had found him? They were on the same side, weren't they? He pushed the box under the chair and slowly went to open the door. As expected, Little Al stood outside.

"Sorry to bother you," Tubbs started a little unsure but very politely. "But, uhm, can I ask you something?" In truth, Tubbs didn't know where to start. Blod seemed familiar, somehow, although now that he was here he didn't really know what to say.

"You can ask me anything you want, Al. I've been waiting for you."

On hearing his mother's pet name for him, Tubbs froze in complete confusion. Who was this man? How did he know his real name?

"Come in so we can close the door on that bloody racket." He turned his back and led the way into the lounge. "Would you like a whisky?"

"Please. Plenty of ice if you've got some."

"Of course," and off went Blod to the kitchen, leaving Tubbs standing in front of the fire. He looked around the sparsely furnished room, and admired the gardener's good taste in music, which was on show on a nearby shelf. His attention was drawn to an old faded photo that lay on the arm of the only chair. Tubbs picked up the picture and was amazed to see his mother's beautiful eyes and gappy-yet-glorious smile staring straight back at him.

Blod returned before Tubbs could gather his thoughts, two glasses in hand and an apprehensive look dawning on his weathered face.

Time stood still as they looked at each other, both unsure what to do next. Blod expected the worst, but instead of a beating, Tubbs calmly took a glass and sat on the floor in the lotus position. His knee screamed bloody murder, but he drowned the pain with a large swig of peaty goodness.

"Who are you, Blod? How do you know my name and how did you know my mother?"

Blod sat in his chair and looked at Tubbs, silently weighing up his options. The ice chimed against the glass, as his hands shook involuntarily; something that did not go unnoticed by Tubbs. He considered the best way to start explaining, but in the end plumped for the truth.

"I was your mother's lover, Al. Her *true* love. Her *soul*mate."

It was now Tubbs's turn to feel his whole body tighten as Blod filled him in, from start to finish. With good reason, the situation didn't feel comfortable to either of them, but in Blod's opinion Tubbs had a right to an explanation. To the truth.

Tubbs listened to each word, although he found it difficult to believe every detail. Contrary to the abundance of evidence, Tubbs considered his mother to be an angel, and hearing about the way in which she betrayed T-Bone – even after all he'd done for her – was hard to take. However, Blod's obvious passion and love for Foxy was undeniable, but something didn't add up…

"…I was with her the night she died…" said the gardener as he neared the end of his story, but he didn't get any further as Tubbs exploded on hearing these words, and within half a breath Blod was nailed to the wall by his windpipe, his feet some six inches off the ground.

"It was YOU!" screamed Tubbs, his spittle soaking Blod's bright red face. The gardener's throat was almost fully sealed and his ability to breathe, and therefore defend himself, was compromised. He struggled for breath. Struggled to answer. But Tubbs had lost it and couldn't stop repeating himself. "It was YOU! It was YOU! It was YOU! It was YOU! It was YOU! It was YOU! It was YOU! It was YOU! It was YOU! It was YOU! It was YOU! It was YOU! It was YOU! It was YOU!"

With one hand holding Blod against the wall, Tubbs turned a little and reached with his free hand to grab the bottle of whisky which stood on the coffee table, with the intention of using it to bludgeon the gardener to death. Slowly. He had his gun in his pocket, of course, but that would be too quick an ending for the man who had ruined his life. But just as his fingers touched the glass, Tubbs noticed the box that had been kicked over – spilling its load – as he tackled the gardener a few moments earlier. He saw more photos of his mother. Letters. Jewellery. A scarf. He loosened his grip and sat on the floor once again to investigate, while Blod fell to the ground in a wheezing heap. After regaining the ability to breathe, Blod spoke quietly to his confused tormentor.

"I have no idea what you're talking about, Al. I *loved* your mother. More than life itself…"

"Sorry," said Tubbs sadly, as Blod picked up the chair and sat down again, grabbing hold of his whisky glass that somehow hadn't been knocked over in the tussle. "Can I read these?"

"Please do. I think they'll prove to you that I'm telling the truth."

And he was right. Foxy's letters explained the situation to Tubbs more effectively than Blod could ever have done himself. It soon became very clear to Tubbs that the man sat in front of him was indeed his mother's lover, her best friend and soulmate. Her *everything*, in fact. The letters also explained how she felt trapped by T-Bone, and scared shitless by his mood-swings. She was grateful for all that he'd done for her, for *them*, but she didn't love him and never had. Foxy felt indebted to T-Bone, which mirrored Tubbs's current relationship with him to some extent. Before her death, Foxy was desperate to leave T-Bone, but was petrified of what would happen to her, to Al and to Andrew if she did.

While reading, Tubbs came to realise that his mother had lost out on her one true chance of happiness. He grabbed a handful of photos from the box and stared at them all individually. He saw Victor as a kitten in one of them, curled up in Foxy's lap. Another showed Blod building the greenhouses – topless, tanned and toned, while yet another must have been taken by self-timer, and showed the happy couple kissing on the deck outside Tubbs's home in Dinas Powys. Then he noticed a very familiar looking ring at the bottom of the box.

"I gave your mam that ring you wear on your pinky finger, the night she was killed. That's the 'his' to her 'hers'. I loved her Al. You've got to believe me. My world ended the same night as hers did and I've been hiding here ever since. Luca's been brilliant, and the rest of the boys. But you're the first person from my past that I've seen since *that* night…

Tubbs looked at Blod, his own tears reflected on the gardener's face.

"I *do* believe you, but this is all a bit of a shock. And I don't know how I'll ever look T-Bone in the eyes again after reading what I've just read…"

"*What*!? You're still in touch with him?"

"Of course. Why? He's been like a father to me…

"Even after…" But Blod stopped talking as he realised the truth.

"Evan after *what*?" asked Tubbs.

Slowly and painfully, Boda's bloodshot peepers opened, dragging their master back to the land of the living-dead. There was a samba band recording a session in his head and the morning sun shone a little too brightly through a slit in the curtains, so he turned to face the other way and came face to face with a naked back in the king-size bed. He remembered the girl. Maya? Milla? Mia? *Whatever*. He smiled. Gently, he started stroking her smooth skin. Maybe he could put his morning glory to good use? His head thumped so he closed his eyes once more and felt her turn to face him. He opened his eyes again, but almost puked on seeing Pennar's face a mere few inches from his own. Pennar was still half-asleep, but Boda had never felt so awake. And sick. He rolled out of the bed and found himself on all-fours, drool dribbling from his slack-jawed-maw. He couldn't remember any details. Which might have been a good thing. He just didn't know. He got up, dressed and got out of there. What happened? Where was the girl? And where did Tubbs spend the night? Boda went to look for him. Before Pennar got up. They had to go home. Now…

The birds chirped in the trees at the start of another day, but Tubbs couldn't identify with their enthusiasm. Not today. His morning yoga session had done little to clear his head. The only thing he could think about were the previous night's revelations – Blod and Foxy's relationship caught him by surprise, but what followed was a million times more stupefying.

Tubbs stood outside the log cabin trying his best to make sense of it all, which would have been difficult at the best of times, but it was impossible after the sleepless night he'd just had.

As Tubbs took a walk around Blod's garden, he realised that it reflected his own patch in many ways. His mother's lover grew organic tomatoes and fruit in a couple of greenhouses in a clearing that enjoyed plenty of sun, and Tubbs also noticed the familiar five-fingered collie leaves that grew wild all over the place. There was even a huge palm tree growing near the cabin, presumably in homage to his lost love. He popped his head into the first greenhouse to see how Blod's toms were coming along and realised at once where his mother got the idea for using seaweed as an insecticide. Tubbs stopped for a while, leaning on a huge oak, and watched a squirrel drinking from a bird bath shaped like a shell. His mind raced as it wrestled with what the gardener had told him during the night.

At last, he was a step closer to catching his mother's killer, and therefore a step closer to fulfilling his contract with T-Bone and getting his hands on the key to his freedom. But there was a lot to do and a lot to deal with before the cell door to his personal hell would open up and let him out…

PERMANENT REMINDER

Like a blind pooch on a thick pile carpet, the night slowly dragged its derrière through the darkness while Petra struggled to get any sleep. She finally gave up around 3 a.m., and by half-past she was sat on her bed, with her back against the headboard, fully dressed and smoking the new day's first fag.

Yesterday's whorewear – namely the short skirt and barely-there vest combo – had been replaced by a tight pair of dark blue jeans and some bright white Lacoste daps that she found in the bottom of the wardrobe; her tits – which were doing their utmost the previous day to escape from their cotton confinement – were in hiding today beneath a light grey Abercrombie hoody, while her hair was tucked beneath a NYC baseball cap; although Petra had never been near an aeroplane, never mind the Big Apple.

While dozing a little earlier, in that cruel no-man's-land between deep sleep and complete consciousness, Vicky had visited her once again, this time invading her dreams. But, instead of carrying a knife, she had something much worse in her possession: the old pro held a syringe full of her own polluted blood, which caused Petra to sit up in bed – eyes wide, eyes wild – the bread-knife held tightly in her grip ready to defend herself, and her heart rattling her ribcage in an attempt to escape its incarceration. With the sweat pouring from her forehead, Petra calmed herself with a ciggy and soon, after her heartbeat had returned to normal, she could hear Vicky heavy-breathing on the other side of the thin dividing wall, while her captors chatted downstairs in the lounge.

Gimp was chillin' on the sofa, his head on the arm in exactly the same place as Petra's tits leaned earlier that afternoon during the taste test. His brain was well and truly fried after another day spent in the company of Barry's biggest speed-freak, and the images that spewed from the telly were a confusion of colours and nonsensical noises. He lit another Marlboro and pulled hard, feeling the smoke flow through his body, before checking the time – 03:24 – and thinking about escaping Vex and joining Vicky in a Valium-assisted land of nod.

Vexl, meanwhile, was sitting in the same position as he was when watching Gimp nail Petra earlier on, staring at the telly with a similar expression on his face. Disgust, that is. Disgust mixed with the expected perplexity that goes hand in hand with the fourth sleepless night in a row. His eyes were as narrow as coin slots, but instead of succumbing to his body and mind's pleading, he reached into his pocket for another slimming pill, sat up slowly and started crushing the tablet on the coffee table.

"Wah did Vickeh seh when yah seen her early on, mon?" Vexl's voice echoed through the ages, causing Gimp to turn his eyes and watch his boss's hand crumbling the chemicals.

"She woz mumblin' summin' abaht everyone leavin' and her bein' stuck ere. I tried to console her like, poor bitch, yuh know, givin it all I aven't left ave I dahlin, but she woz avin none of it like. Babblin on, doin my ead in if truff be told so in ve end I gave her four fackin vals and sweet as a nut, she's snorin like a pig in no time. I nevah known her to be violent like vat in all vese years. She's good as gold, you knows 'at. Got me finkin vat me fackin ve new girl probably didn't help matters. Didn't help *her* innit, cos I fackin luvved it like…" Gimp's words flowed fast, but when he stopped, he didn't have the faintest idea what he had just said. He *had* to sleep. Right now. Before it was too late; before he'd find himself beyond the tipping point where he'd be awake forever.

He reached into his pocket and grabbed a small plastic bottle, opened the top and poured eight blue pills into the palm of his hand. Would 80mg be enough to get him to sleep? Gimp didn't know the answer. In fact, he didn't really know anything anymore.

Vexl looked up from the lines he'd cut on the coffee table and noticed at once what Gimp was holding in his hand.

"Don even t'ink abaht it, Gimpmon!"

"Fack you Vex, I gotta sleep like. I can't go on like vis…" Gimp said, before chucking the tablets down his throat and seeing them off with a swig of lager. Vexl shook his head in absolute disgust.

"Yah battybwoy bag-o-wire!" He hissed as Gimp got up unsteadily and fucked off to bed, before rolling a crisp twenty between his thumb and forefinger and hoovering both lines up his hooter.

Petra's whole body tensed on hearing the footsteps climbing the stairs but drew some comfort from the blade she held tightly in her hand. Her suitcase was packed and waiting for her by the door. All she needed now was a tiny window of opportunity. She breathed a huge sigh of relief when she heard the door to Vicky's bedroom creak open as Gimp joined the skeletal skank beneath the bedcovers.

She lit another cigarette and pulled hard to ease the adrenalin. *Two down, one to go.*

With the telly spewing nothing but reruns, shopping channels and early editions of the news in his general direction, Vexl sat in his chair grinding his teeth and staring into oblivion, if not beyond. His mind was empty, yet full of chaos. Nothing made sense anymore.

The first light of the new day – although Vexl didn't know *which* day it was – infiltrated the lounge through a gap in the curtains and for some unknown reason the pimp had the unexpected urge to see dawn break down on the beach. Although he'd spent the majority of the last decade in this house located within half a click of the coast, Vexl couldn't remember the last time he actually touched the sand. However, considering his state of mind, he could have been building sandcastles there yesterday and he wouldn't have been any wiser.

He struggled to his feet, opened the curtains and welcomed the sight of the light grey dawn beyond the window, sat down again, rolled a huge spliff containing skunkweed and slimming pills, turned off the TV, got up again, pocketed the joint, grabbed his jacket and left the house. By now the early pre-dawn light had turned the world into a life-size pastel landscape, and apart from the darkness that permanently resided within him, Vexl almost felt alive.

In fact, he felt *too* alive and by the end of the street he was shivering. He needed a proper coat to warm his shrivelling shell – the thin black leather longcoat didn't come close to warming his cockles. The amphetamines had picked the flesh from his bones long ago and he now felt like a lizard in a snowstorm. He turned and headed for home, tutting and trembling as he went.

Petra slipped off the bed on hearing the front door open and stepped lightly to the window, where she peeked through the curtains and watched Vexl walk down the garden path, past his car, down the street and out of sight.

She dropped her half-finished fag into the glass of water on the bedside table before gliding over to her case and opening the door without making a sound. On tiptoes, she sneaked past Vicky's room – where the freak-show-lovers were snoring in harmony in the spunk-stained bed – and made her way down the stairs as quietly as she could. Although she knew that Vexl wasn't here, her heart was still beating at a thousand bpm, and with her case in one hand and the bread-knife in the other, she opened the door, sneaked a peek and stepped outside.

With his head down and his shoulders hunched against the cold, Vexl opened the gate and heard the front door to his home close before looking up to see Petra standing on the doorstep, dressed casually and making her escape. With her case in one hand and a knife in the other, his body heated up instantly as they both stood there, stock still, facing each other in the front garden.

Petra stared at her living-breathing nightmare, let go of her suitcase and tightened her grip on the bread-knife. Vexl smiled, which caused her blood to freeze. Victory was her only option; the alternative wasn't worth considering.

"Yah wannah piece oh I, girlee?" Vexl mocked her, but Petra didn't say a word – she wasn't going to waste an ounce of energy talking to her tormentor.

Vexl looked down at her, his nostrils flaring like a raging bull's. A milk float hummed past the scene on the street in front of the brothel, but Petra barely noticed – she was concentrating fully on the one obstacle that stood between her and her freedom.

"Wassa mattah girlee, yah nah like yah new job, yah new home?"

Once again, Petra ignored what came out of Vexl's mouth – not that she understood much of what he said anyway – which made the pimp unzip his coat and reach for the handle of his favourite knife, which lay in wait in the holster under his armpit. But, for the first time ever perhaps – as long as Vexl could remember anyway – the blade caught on the catch as he pulled it clear, which gave Petra the chance to take advantage and act. As Vexl took his eyes off the prize and turned his attention to freeing his knife, Petra stepped to him and planted the bread-knife in his upper arm, anchoring it deep between his bicep and shoulder. Vexl howled in pain and staggered backwards with the knife still sticking out of him. Three seagulls swooped over the scene, screeching in response to Vexl's scream. He wailed in agony but regained his balance and stared menacingly at Petra while slowly and carefully pulling the knife out of his own flesh, grinding his teeth in response to the almost unbearable pain. Once out, Vexl launched the knife and it landed in next door's gardens – well out of harm's way.

Without a knife, Petra was almost without hope. The only thing she could do now was run. Unfortunately, due to the fact that Vexl stood in her way, she didn't get very far. In fact, she didn't get anywhere at all as the pimp tackled her with his unwounded shoulder, causing her to fall to the ground in a winded heap.

Petra lay on the garden path, struggling for breath; while Vexl stood above her, smiling. After all, one of the best thing about his vocation, his calling, was beating the shit out of some ungrateful whore from time to time; especially when there was absolutely no threat of a comeback, like in this case.

He re-hooked the holster catch beneath his armpit and glanced at his wound, which was now dripping blood all over the floor, before bending down slowly and extracting a cut-throat razor from a special slot he'd had inserted in his right boot. This was the perfect tool for what he had in mind. Crouching down, he turned Petra – who had stopped writhing and was now completely still – to face him as a couple of gulls cheered him on from the roof of the house behind him. With Petra on her back seemingly unconscious, he straddled her, using his knees to lock her arms by her side, just in case she was bluffing.

Despite her obliviousness, Vexl whispered in her ear as he pulled the blade slowly down her left cheek, completing half of his intended flesh graffiti within seconds.

"I'm gonnah scah yah widda lettah vee, so everee time yah see yah reflection in dah mirrah, windah or a back ah spoon, you'll t'ink ah me…"

As well as feeling the blade cutting her, Petra heard everything that Vexl said, as she wasn't unconscious in any way. She was acting. Just like yesterday and almost every other day during her young life. Although, even she'd have to admit that acting had never been this painful.

By playing dead, she hoped that Vexl would loosen his grip, lose his concentration or become complacent, which in turn would give her a chance to escape. And sure enough, that chance came shortly after he'd finished the first incision, when his left leg cramped up and forced him to stand in order to stretch his calf muscle.

The pain ripped through his leg. He looked down at Petra, happy to have scarred her perfect skin and ruined her looks forever. She deserved all she got; especially considering everything he'd already done for her. He leaned on his left leg, stretching out until the cramp faded. His shoulder was still streaming blood and he felt a little faint, although that could have been the drugs and the lack of sleep.

Petra felt the weight lift and heard Vexl cursing and groaning - whether from the pain in his wounded shoulder or some other cause, she didn't know. Slyly, she took a peep and saw her chance – after all, it was *literally* staring her in the face.

If Vexl's shoulder and calf conspired to cause him pain, they were both dwarfed by what he felt when Petra's right foot connected squarely with his scrotum and sent him flying forward towards the front door and the concrete path. Petra got to her feet, turned and came face to face with Vexl's behind, as its owner desperately tried to get to his feet. He hadn't got further than all fours, which offered her the perfect bull's eye and she didn't need a second invitation, so she kicked him in exactly the same spot, which caused him to squeal and sprawl towards the doorstep.

As Vexl struggled to recover from the double blow, the only thing Petra could think of was escaping. But when Vexl started getting up, she knew she had to do more than that. She looked around for a weapon and found the perfect warhead close to hand…

Vexl dragged himself to his feet, using the doorstep as leverage and the gable to grab on to. But before he could regain his composure and balance, Petra hit him on the back of the head with her suitcase, which she swung like a baseball bat, causing his face to smash into the pebble-dashed wall in front of him. His nose shattered, his skull cracked and Petra watched as Vexl slowly fell to the floor, dragging his face down the wall and ending in a lifeless heap on the path in front of her. Petra stared at what she had done, before leaving the scene in a hurry, dragging her freshly-stained suitcase behind her.

Before reaching the end of the street, Petra had convinced herself that she'd killed Vexl. Deservedly so, maybe, but it would still be enough to see her locked up for a long time. She stopped when she turned the corner to catch her breath and wipe her bloody cheek with a tissue.

After regaining her composure, she peeked around the bend just in time to see Vexl shuffling towards her, bumping into parked cars and shouting at the top of his voice as if he was drunk or retarded – possibly both.

As her tormentor tumbled and tripped over an invisible obstacle, it was now Petra's turn to smile. She grabbed her suitcase and turned on her heels, walking briskly back towards the Safari Inn. Petra retraced the route they took to Barry the previous day and aimed for Dow Corning, Dinas Powys and Cardiff beyond. She looked over her shoulder every fifty yards or so as she expected Vexl and Gimp to be on her tail, but thankfully there was no sign of them.

Forty-five minutes of brisk-walking later, she neared the outskirts of Dinas Powys as the lethargy, at last, caught up and overtook her. She needed somewhere to rest for a little while, to recharge her batteries before pushing on to the capital, and after detouring through some playing fields and jumping over a crumbling stone wall, she found shelter in a wild and overgrown garden on the edge of the village, in the company of a toothless old cat.

FOX HUNT

Wednesday. Seven o'clock. The Safari Inn's empty car park. In fact: it wasn't *quite* seven o'clock, more like six fifty-seven; while the car park wasn't *totally* empty either. In the far corner, melting effortlessly into the early shadows of this humid summer evening, a lone car was parked. In the vehicle, hunched over the steering wheel, sat a lonely figure watching the motel's main entrance through emotionless eyes. Clad head-to-toe in army surplus gear – khaki trousers, military green jacket - his long grey-speckled hair and handlebar moustache somehow didn't sit comfortably with the mint-green Ford Escort he drove. This Bandit would have been more at home astride a steed of steel, but he had good reason for coming here in a stolen set of wheels. He was trying to blend in, to be anonymous – something that would have been impossible if he'd have arrived on the back of his chopper.

What the fuck is she doing coming to a place like this? He thought, staring at the sorry looking establishment, while pulling on a pair of see-through latex gloves. As expected in a motel called the Safari Inn, there were jungle motifs everywhere – zebra print doors, leopard skin curtains – but the only wildlife on show were the drunks that frequented the pub next door, who popped out from time to smoke, shout and walk into things. Right on cue, he watched as a red-nosed vagrant left the pub and stumbled slowly out of sight, his light trousers sporting a dark wet stain. Pint or piss? Who knew? Who cared?

With the cold steel hanging heavily in his shoulder holster, part of him still hoped that the love of his life wouldn't show; but unfortunately for her, him, her lover and son, he watched with great sadness as a taxi pulled up and dropped her off some fifty yards from where he sat…

Foxy stepped from the back seat of the taxi onto the puke-soaked pavement, bent down, paid the driver and told him to keep the change. Before entering the motel, she quickly scanned the vicinity, but saw nothing that added to her apprehension. She was very nervous tonight; far more than usual. And although she'd been seeing Andrew behind T-Bone's back for more than a year, meeting in a motel gave the act a sinister edge somehow.

She pushed through the zebra-print portal and came face to face with the hippopotamus-like hotelier, sat behind the reception desk with one eye on *The Price is Right*, which was blaring from a portable black and white TV, and the other on a half-eaten plate of Clark's pie and chips that his equally obese wife had served up some ten minutes earlier.

Foxy coughed to get his attention, before asking for Mr Jones's room, and after acquiring the answer, she turned on her heels and aimed towards her lover's arms, while the manager watched her go, wondering what a nice piece like that was doing in a shithole like this.

Blod lay on the soft mattress regretting the fact that he hadn't checked the motel out beforehand. He wished they were meeting somewhere a little more classy. A *lot* more classy, in fact. With far less leopard-print. He chose the place on the advice of Dee and Lance, two young labourers who helped him from time to time when something major needed doing in one of the gardens he serviced. But lying there, recalling the conversation, it hit him that the little fuckers were taking the piss; and fair play to them, they'd fuckin' done him good and proper this time.

The bed sheets were stained with the room's recent history, and the fact that you could hire them by the hour did nothing to ease his mind. The bamboo wallpaper was yellowing and peeling and might have been considered a good idea a decade earlier. Or not. He stared at the artexed ceiling, and marvelled at the shoddy workmanship, while hoping that Foxy wouldn't walk away from the place as soon as she set eyes on it.

The lovers hadn't spent any time together for a week – the longest they'd been apart since the beginning of their relationship – and Blod couldn't wait to feast on her sexual smorgasbord as soon as she entered the room; *if* she entered the room. He'd kiss her from head to toe, and back again, paying close attention to her inner thighs, belly, breasts, neck and earlobes, before turning the bed into a flange-fluid-filled paddling-pool with some tongue-twisting clit-cajoling.

And just as his cock reached half-mast in response to his imagination, there was a knock on the door. Blod bounded off the bed and on opening the door, he was practically raped by his lover, who wrestled him to the mattress like a sex-starved Amazonian, before ripping off his clothes, pulling her knickers to one side and sliding him in effortlessly, with no word of greeting. But who needed words, when actions screamed this loudly?

Following a few minutes of bedroom-Buckaroo, they'd both ejaculated and added to the bed sheets' collection of stains, before untangling from each other's arms and lying back to inspect the ceiling together, like lovers do.

After heavy breathing for a little while and generally recovering from the rigorous workout, Blod turned to look at his lover, and said the first words of the evening (not counting 'Yes! Yes!', 'Fuck me hard!' and 'IIIIIIIIII'm commmmmmmmmmmmming!', of course).

"And who exactly are you again?" he asked.

"Mzzzz Jones," Foxy answered, laughing and lighting a menthol cigarette and blowing the smoke towards Blod's face. They both laughed, before Blod produced two jade rings from the bedside drawer and held them up for Foxy to see.

"What's 'at?"

"Is that a trick question or something?"

"Don't be a dick, Andrew. I obviously know *what* they are… but… oh… you know what I mean!"

"Well, one of them's for you and the other one's for me…"

"His and hers!" Foxy exclaimed, before pinching Blod's cheeks and adding: "That's *soooooo* cute!"

"Don't take the piss," he responded, slightly miffed but determined not to spoil the moment. "They're both made with jade, which represents faithfulness…"

Foxy laughed, before stopping herself on seeing the hurt in Andrew's eyes.

"Sorry, luv," began Foxy, although she couldn't completely stop herself from laughing. "It's just… well… you have to admit that handing me, your illicit lover, a ring representing faithfulness in the Safari Inn is just a little bit on the funny side."

"I'll admit that," answered Blod, with a smile. "But my point is this: I know you can never leave T-Bone and spend your life with me, but these rings represent my love for you, my commitment and complete dedication to you. I'm yours forever, Lisa, and if that means sharing you with someone else, then fuck it, I can live with that. I'm just glad you're part of my life in some way. I love you with all my heart. And then some…"

Foxy choked the menthol in the ashtray, before Blod placed the ring on the middle finger of her left hand. She returned the favour, before they embraced. While hugging her true love, the tears rolled down her face – a mixture of elation and sadness. Sadness that she hadn't found Andrew sooner; and happiness that she'd met him at all.

"What's *that*?" she asked, referring to the posh-looking bottle that stood next to the bedside lamp.

"What?" asked Blod, turning to see what she was talking about. "Oh, yes, champers. I'd forgotten about that what with all the... you know... I was going to get some ice from reception..."

"Well chop-chop then!" Foxy ordered. "I simply refuse to drink warm champagne!" So Blod dressed quickly, kissed her hard on the lips and left the room.

"Curly blonde girl. Came in about ten minutes ago. What room's she in? It'll be under Mr and Mrs Jones, I believe."

The motel manager looked up from the dregs of his supper, more than a little annoyed that this moustachioed mug was disturbing the climax of his favourite game show.

"Can't tell you, butt. Against motel policy like..."

"Would this help in any way?" asked the stranger, while slipping a crisp tenner across the desk's dusty surface. The manager looked at the note, then back at the man.

"It helps, yes. But it's not *quite* enough to get you that sort of information..." The stranger considered going for his gun and cutting to the chase, but didn't want any trouble. Not yet, anyway...

"How about this then?" He added a twenty to the ten, which made the manager's eyes light up a little – he could get a colour TV for that sort of cash – although his answer didn't please.

"Still not *quite* enough...

Unfortunately for him, the stranger was of the opinion that it was in fact *more* than enough, so he reached over the desk, grabbed the greedy bastard by his ears and hair, lifted him out of his seat and dragged him halfway across the desk.

"Don't take the fuckin' piss now, fatboy," he hissed. "There's thirty quid by there, I suggest you tell me what I want to know and take it. Either that or I take it back, beat the shit out of you and go find her myself. So, I repeat, *what room*?"

"S-s-s-seventeen..." the manager stuttered.

"Thank you," growled the hunter, before cracking the fat man's face against the desk and pocketing the cash.

Blod reached reception and found the manager struggling to get to his feet. His nose was broken and what was really needed was a pulley, but Blod did his best and within a minute or two he was back in his chair, breathing heavily, reaching for his Superkings and checking the desk as if he'd lost something.

"You all right now?"

"Aye. Thanks for the hand. Appreciate it."

"What happened – your nose? It's bleeding. Could be broken."

"Uh… blackout… happens sometimes… I got this condition like… I'll get the missus to look at it now…"

"Ok. Have you lost something?"

"Uhm. Nah. Nah, not really. It'll turn up I'm sure…"

"Ok. If you're sure…"

"Yeah. Can I help *you* with something?"

"I need an ice bucket…" The manager looked at Blod as if he was mental. An ice bucket? In the Safari Inn? What a fucking joke. A bucket – no problem. Ice – of course. But an *ice bucket* – no chance. Blod smiled, realising the ridiculousness of his request.

"I don't have one here like, but if you go to the pub next door, tell 'em Big Dave sent you, I'm sure they'll help you out…"

The light knock on the door awoke Foxy from her post-coital snooze, and she got up in a daze and glided nakedly towards the sound. She had discarded her clothes after Blod had left, with the intention of getting right back down to business as soon as he returned. She slowly opened the door and was ready to give Andrew a little light grief for forgetting his key and disturbing her slumber, but the huge hand that clasped her throat was proof enough that this wasn't her lover; this was her worst nightmare.

She was lifted off her feet, and thrown backwards onto the bed by the Angel of Death, where she bounced and broke her fall on the flimsy wall, denting the plaster in the process. She lay in a heap on the dirty carpet – winded, confused and frothing with fear. She sobbed as she grabbed the bed sheets and wrapped them around herself, trying to mask the truth – but it was too late for that. *Far* too late, in fact.

T-Bone could smell the sex in the bedroom's stale air. He stared at Foxy, writhing and sobbing pathetically in front of him. He knelt down and checked under the bed, his pistol cocked and ready for action. He *had* to be here. But where? He opened the wardrobe. Empty.

"Where is he?"

"Who?"

"*Who?* Don't take the piss, Foxy! *Him*. Whoever *he* is." Foxy thought of Andrew. He'd be back in a minute, and then what? She couldn't begin to imagine, but knew it wouldn't be good. Foxy was quite confident that she could wriggle out of this situation with nothing more than a lesson learnt from the back of T-Bone's hand, but she knew that her lover would be dealt with in a different way.

"He's *gone*," she said, turning on the taps for maximum effect. "He said he couldn't go on like this. Wanted me all to himself. I told him I couldn't leave you, so he went…"

T-Bone shook his head in utter disgust. His heart ached in response to her blatant lies. Silently and sadly, he lifted the gun and pointed it towards her, before pausing to reach into his pocket for a silencer and attaching it.

Blod bounced back towards the grimy love-nest with an ice bucket held in both hands, but as he neared room seventeen, he could see that the door was ajar, even from the other end of the corridor. He didn't think anything of it and continued on his way. Foxy was probably in the shower or something, and left the door open for him to return. But, just as he was poised to enter, he froze. He could hear a man's voice inside, inquiring about his whereabouts.

His heart galloped, thundering between his ears, but regardless of that he could still hear what was being said on the other side; and although he couldn't *see* the man's face, he'd recognise his boss's voice anywhere.

Foxy was well and truly in the shit. T-Bone didn't believe a word she had to say, and with his gun pointed straight at her she could see the hatred and fury simmering deep within his slate-grey eyes. She knew from experience that he hated being crossed, betrayed, especially by a friend, which did nothing for her hopes of escaping from the Safari Inn with her life intact.

She prayed that Andrew wouldn't return. Or at least, that he'd return, hear T-Bone's voice and run. Head for the hills and save himself from the inevitable doom that awaited him here.

"I gave you *everything*, Foxy. And *this* is how you thank me."

Foxy looked up, but had nothing to say. The answer, after all, was written all over the room – the champers, the discarded clothes, and her nakedness.

"Since when?"

"Since when *what*?"

"Since when has… *this*… been going on? Since when have you been fucking *him* and deceiving *me*?" Foxy stared into oblivion. How could she answer truthfully without inviting T-Bone to pull the trigger? "And no bullshit now, Foxy. No more lies…"

"I've *never* loved you, Tony," she gave it to him straight, and the fact that she used his real name for once made the revelation all the more cruel. "Not *really*, anyway. I mean, I'm grateful for all you've done for me, and for Al, but that's as far as it goes. I'm glad that Al found a good father figure, and I know this must look bad, but I've found someone I truly love and…"

"Why didn't you tell me?"

Foxy laughed out loud but stopped when she saw T-Bone's grip tighten on the gun.

"How *could* I? Look at your reaction. You're too possessive. Too controlling. Too selfish. Self-absorbed. You want to control every*one* and every*thing* around you. You can't stand being contradicted and no one's allowed to answer you back. You're a control freak. Always have been, always will. And you only brought me the hou…"

"*Exactly*! I brought you that house to give you some independence…"

"Ha! What a joke! That house made it impossible for me to *ever* leave you. It caged me even further. But that *was* your intention. Wasn't it?"

"No…"

"Don't deny it! You can't accept it when someone refuses to play your game. You're petrified of losing control. Petrified of looking weak…"

T-Bone cocked the hammer, which silenced Foxy in full flow, but instead of pulling the trigger and doing what he came here to do; he lowered his head and gathered his thoughts. The truth hurt, but not half as much as the betrayal. He didn't want to kill her, but could see no other way. *He thought of* Al. He cherished their relationship more than life itself. But he *had* to kill her. She had left him no choice. However, when he looked up to face Foxy once again, possibly for the final time, he came face to face with a Magnum .44, which she held in her trembling hands, pointed right at his chest. He raised his eyebrows but he had to admire her balls. The sight took him straight back to the alley where they first met. This wasn't the first time she'd pointed a gun at him, although unlike that night, he now knew that she could never shoot him. It simply wasn't in her nature. T-Bone lifted his gun; his hands steady with experience, his heart turned to stone.

"I'll ask you again, and this is your last chance – *where* is he?"

Blod held his breath on the other side of the door, still paralysed with fear.

"I *told* you…"

"C'mon now Foxy, we both know that was a load of cobblers."

"We had a massive row and off he went. That's the *truth*…"

"The truth? You don't know the meaning of the word!" And that's when Blod heard a gun click. The hammer falling on an empty chamber, that is. Followed by a disappointing little clunk. He was hugely relieved and almost burst into the room to face his boss but it soon dawned on him – when he heard T-Bone chuckle – that the situation wasn't quite as he had pictured it.

"Foxy, Foxy, Foxy," tutted the bandit. "You're a piece of fucking work, you know that. You broke my heart, and now you're trying to *kill* me." While T-Bone smiled, Foxy sobbed and stared at her gun through the mist. T-Bone shook his head, took a deep breath and pulled the trigger…

T-Bone shot the love of his life only once. The shot went straight through her heart, spraying the room, and everything in it, with blood. However, this didn't kill her instantly. For a short while, T-Bone stared as the life drained slowly from her – the blood eventually gurgling up and out of her mouth as she lay on her side in a final pose.

Tears streamed silently down his cheeks, but they soon dried as he regained control. She was so right about him. No one crossed him. Ever.

He crouched down by her side, looked in her eyes and plucked the gun from her grasp; which was when he noticed the jade ring. Before leaving the scene to hunt his second victim, he slipped the ring off her finger and placed it, along with the gun, in his jacket pocket. They'd both be something for Al to remember her by.

Blod's heart almost burst free of its rib cage when he heard the gunshot. He almost screamed but luckily his brain caught up with his larynx just in time to avert that near-disaster. His next instinct was to burst into the room and beat the shit out of T-Bone, but he knew that would be an unfair fight as he didn't possess a weapon of any kind.

He could hear the Bandit mumbling to himself on the other side of the door, followed by some riffling, and although his head was shot and his heart would never be whole again, he knew it was time to leave. Or at least it was time to hide, before T-Bone found him and sent him to the same place as Foxy, or maybe somewhere a whole lot worse.

He turned and looked up and down the narrow corridor. His options were limited to one, and even that one wasn't close to being failsafe. Some five yards away, in the opposite direction to the exit, stood a vending machine, so Blod hot-footed it up the hallway and hid on the other side. Standing there, trying not to make a sound, Blod knew that if T-Bone chose to come this way, the game would be over in an instant.

He heard the door to room seventeen creak open. He held his breath and closed his eyes, then heard T-Bone's steps going the other way, away from his hiding place. His spirits rose for a split-second, before he remembered what had just happened. He waited there until he heard the exit door open and close, then sneaked a peak and stepped out with the intention of fleeing into the night through the nearest open window.

But, there was no way he could go without saying goodbye to Lisa, although he'd regret doing so for the rest of his life. This wasn't the way he wanted to remember her – a corpse, a cadaver, her face covered in blood, her lifeless eyes staring into oblivion.

He stepped into the room, around the bed and looked down at his one true love. The tears streamed from his eyes as he fought to catch his breath. In the near distance, he could hear doors banging and raised voices as T-Bone searched the motel in vain. Blod kneeled down by Foxy's side, held her still-warm hand and stroked her hair. He noticed that her ring had gone, and looked for it quickly under the bed, before his blood ran cold once again on hearing the door to the corridor slam open and some seriously heavy footsteps coming his way. Blod slid under the bed as T-Bone banged his way up the corridor, kicking in doors and swearing blindly. He tried not to breathe.

T-Bone cursed to himself. He should have searched the room properly before careering around the motel in search of his quarry. The cops would be closing in already and he needed to get back to Rudry, burn the car and his clothes. But first, he had a job to finish…

There was no sign of him anywhere, but then again, T-Bone didn't actually know who he was looking for. He could be any one of the other Safari Inn residents, although T-Bone was somehow convinced he'd see the heartbreak in his eyes or sense the huge void in his soul. He returned to room seventeen and stood at the door breathing heavily as his eyes scanned the scene one last time. He considered having another peek under the bed and in the wardrobe, just to make sure, but with his nerves shot to pieces and the adrenalin mugging his other senses, the wail of a siren nearby made the decision for him. Casanova would have to wait.

Blod could hear T-Bone huffing and puffing by the open door.

Time stood still for a little while, before kick-starting once again when the Bandido walked away, as the sirens neared the scene of the crime. He slipped out from under the bed, wiped every surface he might have touched with a towel, collected his stuff and glanced at his lover's cooling cadaver once more before following her murderer into the night. Through the window of the fire exit door, he watched T-Bone make his escape in a Ford Escort, tyres screeching on the car park's summer-dry surface.

As he bounded past the pub next door, aiming for the car that he'd parked around the corner, he was glad that he gave a false name when booking the room and that he'd paid up front using cash. He had no real idea either as to why he parked the car on a nearby street, as opposed to the motel car park, but in hindsight it was a stroke of genius. As he unlocked the door and slid behind the wheel, three squad cars roared past, sirens blaring, lights flashing, but too late to do anything of use.

Without warning, the reality of what had happened hit him hard, which caused the tears to flow like they'd never done before. But even as they streamed down his cheeks, he knew that he had to put his emotions to one side for the moment. His grief would have to wait. He had to make his escape. Right now. He pulled himself together, started the engine and glided into the night after waiting for another pair of pandas to fly past.

Fortunately for Blod, T-Bone didn't take much notice of his domestic staff, especially the gardeners who hardly ever set foot in the house and therefore rarely crossed paths with the master. Every Friday, he'd leave their wages – cash in hand, of course – in envelopes on the kitchen table, and let them get on with their duties with minimal input and interference. What this meant was that there was no way that T-Bone could follow a paper trail back to Blod's front door. And in another stroke of luck, no one – except for Foxy – even knew his real name, never mind used it. He was universally known as Blod, that's how he introduced himself to everyone.

He drove from Barry to Grangetown, where his home – a grotty little bedsit – was located. Within twenty minutes, he'd loaded the car with everything he needed – clothes, records, books, photo albums, letters, official documents and not much else. Luckily, he'd cleared his stuff from Foxy's house in Dinas Powys a few days earlier, in preparation for Little Al moving in, which meant that he was pretty much in the clear where T-Bone was concerned. There weren't even any photos of him left at Foxy's as she'd insisted that he take the lot in case Al saw them and started asking questions.

He sat in his car and pondered his next move. There was only one place he could think of to go: Galway, on Ireland's Atlantic coast, where an aunt and a few cousins lived. He'd been there many times during his life and couldn't think of a better place to disappear. He headed west, but didn't get any further than Ceredigion…

A BAD START TO THE DAY
(PART 1, 2 & 3)

"GOOD MORNING," was Blod's thoughtless greeting when he joined Tubbs on the raised deck outside his log cabin, holding a cup of coffee in each hand and a long-forgotten emotion deep within his soul; namely a renewed thirst for revenge.

Tubbs looked up from where he was sitting on a rickety wooden bench, overlooking this little Eden. He said nothing.

"Sorry. I don't know why I said that…" Blod sat down, smiled weakly.

"No worries. Thanks for the coffee. I need it too; I hardly slept a wink."

"That's no surprise after what I told you. I'd say sorry if it wasn't for the fact that I'm glad you've finally heard the truth."

"Me too. Sort of." Blod nodded to show that he understood Tubbs's uncertainty.

"Come on," ordered the gardener, after they'd both finished their drinks. "Breakfast," he explained as he left the deck, and when Tubbs entered the dwelling his nostrils started twitching in response to the wonderful aroma that filled the place. "Chai," came Blod's almost psychic explanation, as the cinnamon, cloves, cardamom and aniseed that simmered in a heavy black cauldron in the kitchen lead him straight back to childhood. His mother loved drinking chai – the house in Dinas Powys often reeked of the stuff – and now Tubbs realised why.

They sat on bar stools in the kitchen, using the worktop as a table, and stared silently out of the window as the morning sun penetrated the trees. But the darkness of Tubbs's internal struggle was in complete contrast to the morning glory outside.

Blod handed Tubbs a large bowl of Bircher muesli as well as a mug of chai, which he lifted at once to his nose to feast on the medley of mixed spices.

"How do you feel, then?" Blod asked, knowing at once that it was a ridiculous question. Tubbs pondered for a while, giving the question far more thought than it deserved. The discomfort floated in the air between them, but then something very strange happened – Tubbs started pouring his heart out.

"I'm a mess, Blod, that's the truth," he started. "I feel as if my guts have been ripped out, kicked around for an hour or two before being reattached by a blind baboon."

Blod smiled. Tubbs didn't.

"This is the third parent I've lost now… I mean, I know T-Bone's not dead… yet… but he might as well be…" He fell silent, but before Blod had the chance to contribute to the conversation, the usually silent and sullen giant was off again.

"I'm totally gutted as well. I can't believe that T-Bone, my dad in every sense except the biological one, could do that to Mam. But what's worse… well, maybe not *worse*, but still pretty fucking sick, is the fact he's looked me in the eye all these years and lied. Over and over again. Nothing but lies. Day after day, year after year…" He paused, drank some chai, appreciated its warmth. "I realise now that he's been controlling me with these lies since the very day Mam died. And that makes me feel like a right twat, I tell you. Not to mention angry…"

Blod nodded, although he had little idea what Al was in fact referring to.

"But regardless of all the stuff you told me last night, I still don't *want* to believe it. I don't want to believe that someone I've loved for so long, someone I've respected, could do such a thing and then bullshit me about it ever since…"

He paused again, gathered his scattered thoughts and ate a mouthful of muesli, but before continuing Blod piped up.

"Unlike him, Al, I haven't lied to you once…"

"I know that. I really do. But I don't *want* to believe it. Not a word. I want to hear it from him. I *have* to hear it from him. He's lied to me for far too long…"

"What have you got in mind?"

"Loads of things. Too much, really. Revenge comes pretty close to the top of the list. But that makes me as bad as him, doesn't it?"

"Not at all. He deserves whatever's coming to him. Whatever you've got in mind. I know that your mother wasn't completely blameless, after all, she *was* having an affair behind his back, but she didn't deserve to die. No way."

"Exactly. So the next question is…"

"How?" Blod butted in.

"Yes. How?"

"Luckily for you, I've been dreaming of this for over a decade, without once thinking the day would come."

"Go on."

"It's simple really…"

"*Simple*! How?"

"A phone call. An invite. A meeting."

"Go on."

"Ok. You give me his phone number. I call him. Introduce myself. Invite him somewhere to discuss the situation. I'll keep it vague. Dangle the bait so to speak. You've got to remember that he's probably been waiting for the chance to finish me off since that night as well. Then, with you hiding somewhere, listening in, I'll guide the conversation towards what happened at the Safari Inn so that you can hear him say it, admit what he did, before stepping out and doing whatever you feel like doing to him…"

Tubbs paused. Considered. Questioned.

"But *why* would he agree to meet you?"

"Because I'm the only one who knows his little secret."

"Not quite, but I get what you're saying. He'll want to finish the job and bury the truth once and for all."

"Exactly! There's no way he *wouldn't* come."

Some hundred miles to the east, Vexl sat on the brothel doorstep, his dreadlocked bonce between his knees, breathing as if he was in labour and watching the blood drip from his nose, pooling crimson on the floor between his feet.

The blood tasted metallic as it collected and clotted at the back of his throat, as if he'd just sucked on a battery or something equally industrial. How long had he been lying unconscious in the gutter, before dragging his sorry ass back here to bleed? Seconds? Maybe. Hours? The same answer. In short, he didn't have a clue.

But although he didn't know *how* exactly he got beaten senseless by a little girl, he did know *who* was to blame for the morning's prison break...

"GIIIIIIIIIIIIIIIIIIIMP!" he shouted.

"GIIIIIIIIIIIIIIIIIIIIIIIIIIIIIIIIIIIIIIIIIIIIIIIIMP!" he spat.

And although the little man was lying no further than five metres from where Vexl sat, there came no answer.

He looked at his car, parked on the street right in front of the house, and thought about getting in and going after Petra, but she could be anywhere by now, and anyway, he didn't even see which direction she went.

"GIIIIIIIIIIIIIIIIIIIIIIIIIIIIIIIIIMP!" he shouted once more, before getting to his feet and going to see where the short cunt was. He went up the stairs and into the bedroom, barging the door with his bloody – and by now numb – shoulder like a drug squad officer on a dawn raid, where he found the odd couple snoring in harmony like something out of a Grimm fairytale gone very badly wrong.

"GIIIIIIIIIIIIIIIIIIMP!" he shouted again, still to no avail, which made his blood go from a fast-simmer to steady boil. Like a man possessed, his red-eyes bulged above his shattered nose, as he watched Gimp continue to sleep, thanks mainly to the sedatives he necked a few hours earlier, and totally unaware of the human hurricane that was about to land on the shore of his sleepy island.

Vexl stepped to the side of the bed and watched Gimp's mouth gargle like a small geyser. Suddenly, the madness that had always been within him exploded to the surface and Vexl mounted the bed and straddled Gimpmon, nailing his arms to the side of his body with his knees, just as he'd done to Petra before the cramp kicked in and she kicked off. As hard as he could, he slapped Gimp across the cheek, but amazingly the little man continued to snooze.

"Bobo wanna cold I up. We see how yuh like dis fuckery," Vexl mumbled, before lashing out at his friend's face with a quick closed-fist combo, that hit the mark and woke him from his slumber. He tried to raise his hands to defend himself against the unexpectedly fierce alarm-call, and panicked wildly when he couldn't move an inch.

"Wha' ve fack are ya doin' Vex? Fackin' hell, you a fackin loony!"

Vexl smiled, his blood-red nose still dripping wildly.

"Wot ve fack appenned to you?"

"Why didnya wake mon? I been a callin!" Vexl spat.

"Wot ya on abaht, Vex? I've been fackin kippin, in I!"

"Ya shouldna eaten dem sweeties mon! It's all ya fault..."

"Wot is? Wot's my fault?"

"She be gone, mon."

"Who?"

"Petra doll. She dun dis to meh!" Gimp laughed on hearing this – not because it was funny, per se, but because it seemed so unlikely, so ridiculous. But Vexl wasn't to know that, and suddenly he had his hunting knife in his hand and before Gimp could react, he'd sliced his cheek twice in quick succession, branding him with a perfect 'V'. Gimp screamed and struggled to break free, which caused Vexl to lose his balance and Vicky to wake up and join in the chorus, before pushing the pimp with all her might, making him fall to the floor in a bloody heap.

Vexl struggled to his feet. Vicky trembled in anticipation of what was to come her way, but Gimp jumped out of bed, wearing nothing but a stained pair of off-white boxer shorts, and stood between the raging dread and the petrified prossie, holding a hand to his cheek, not quite believing what had just happened. His head was surprisingly clear, considering the amount of Vals he had taken for his night-cap.

"Don't even fackin fink abaht it!" he hissed at Vexl.

"Ahm nah gonna touch her bwatty bwoy, na cam on, we goin aftah da ho…"

"Like fack we are! Ya cut me like one ov ya bitches!" Before answering, Vexl looked him up and down, from his feet to his head and back again.

"Yah *is* one o' mah bitches, bobo! Nah gyet yah threads ahn let's go!"

"I ain't goin' nowhere wiv you, mate. Look at ve fackin state o' ya. Ya don't even know what day it is, never mind which way she went!"

"Dehn why yah wearin dem clothes bwoy?"

It was Gimp's turn to pause before answering this time. He pulled his trousers up and put on yesterday's T-shirt, before slipping on his shoes and standing to face Vexl. His cheek stung as if it'd just been buggered by a hundred bees, but he wasn't going to let his old-friend and new-nemesis know that. He grabbed a fag from the packet in his pocket, lit it and blew the smoke in the face of the fool standing before him.

"I'm outta ere, mate. Gone. No longer your little Gimpmon. No longer your slave. No longer…"

"Yah nah goin nowhere, battybwoy. Yah owe me, don't be forgettin dat…"

"I owe you shit, Vexl. Wot ya just did, wot ya just said, that's fackin quits you ask me."

Vexl stood in stunned silence as Gimp pushed past him and headed for the door. The pimp looked at the blood on the pillow, and then at Vicky trembling beneath the bed sheets.

Before leaving the room, Gimp turned and looked at the mess. Vicky was wailing as she watched him go, realising for the first time that she loved the little man more than life itself.

"I'll be back for my stuff later," said Gimp, with new found authority.

"What about *me*, Gimp?" Vicky asked, between sobs. "What about *me*?" He looked at her with a small smile tickling the corners of his mouth.

After a lonely breakfast in his massive house, T-Bone's footsteps echoed off the walls of the hallway as he headed for the front door. He stepped out into the glorious morning, and took a deep breath before moving on. He slowly meandered through the grounds, making his way to his office in the clubhouse on the other side of the estate, stopping from time to time to listen to a woodpecker or to watch a hawk hang-gliding in the sky above his little piece of heaven. He almost stood on a sunbathing adder, who had set up camp in the middle of the path, but managed to side-step it at the last second, before watching the resident heron coming in to land in the shallows of the well-hidden natural lake that formed the centrepiece of the estate. He smiled to himself, and appreciated the fat slice of luck that life had dealt him.

The clubhouse was empty when he eventually got there. He unlocked the front door and walked through the public area that was more like a bombsite than a bar that morning, following last night's carnage as one of the biker gang's young bucks celebrated his thirtieth birthday in the traditional fashion – top shelf, top off and a top laugh. As he opened the door marked 'private', he heard a car pull up outside and turned to watch the cleaners arrive to take care of the muck.

The Olbas oil hit him as soon as he opened the door to his office and he promptly opened every window, before filling the kettle to prepare a pot of strong Colombian coffee. As the water began to boil, the phone rang. He picked it up and fully expected to hear a short pause, followed by an Indian accent attempting to sell him something or other. Somehow they knew he arrived in the office around this time and would always call and catch him; but that wasn't the case today – today's call was far more interesting.

"Anthony?" the voice asked, which got his full attention. Only one person ever called him by his given name, and she hadn't been around to do so for a long time.

"Who is this?"

"A blast from the past…"

"What?"

"A blast from the past."

"And what *exactly* does that mean?" asked T-Bone, although he had an inkling as to who was on the other end of the line. He'd been expecting this call for ages…

"Does the Safari Inn mean anything to you?"

"Who are you?"

"I'll take that as a yes…"

"Look, if you don't tell me, I'll hang up. I haven't got time to play silly-buggers. Now who are you and what do you want?"

"Let me put it this way – I'm the man you failed to find that night in Barry…"

"What night in Barry?"

"You know *exactly* what night I'm referring to."

"Remind me."

"The night you killed Foxy. And don't even pretend that you don't remember."

T-Bone paused and watched the kettle reaching boiling point, carefully considering his next move.

"What do you want?"

"A meeting."

"Why?"

"To discuss things."

"To discuss *what*?"

"What you did. What I know. And where we go from here."

"Where do you want to meet?"

"Ceredigion…"

"An address would be useful, Ceredigion's quite a big place, don't you know?"

Blod ignored the sarcasm, and continued with what he'd rehearsed.

"I'll be waiting for you in the Brynhoffnant Arms car park, on the A487 by the turn-off to Aberporth. From there, I'll take you somewhere a little more private. I don't want any trouble, mind, so don't bring a gun… or any company. I'll be watching you arrive and if anything's amiss I'll disappear once again. This has been playing on my mind for many years, but I'm prepared to keep silent forever, for a small price of course. Otherwise…"

T-Bone couldn't quite believe his luck – the only person who could connect him with Foxy's murder had contacted him, served himself up on a plate in fact, complete with salad garnish and a large portion of curly fries. What a complete idiot! He'd go along with whatever he suggested, but when they were alone, he'd finish it once and for all.

THE WRONG ANSWER

LOADING TEN kilos of top quality skunkweed into the back of his best friend's car would normally have made Boda very happy indeed. But this morning, coming down hard from last night's mammoth intake of class-A drugs and hard liquor, and not forgetting the psychological trauma experienced on waking up naked in bed with his new buddy, Pennar, the undertaking did nothing but make him sweat a lot and feel a little sick.

Remnants of last night's festivities could be seen everywhere – empty cans and bottles strewn on the floor, an unconscious couple snoozing under a tarp over by the still-smouldering bonfire – but, as Boda loaded the bricks of weed into the boot of Tubbs's car round the back of the barn, none of the casualties were aware of what was going on.

The trio – Boda, Tubbs and Tulip, one of Blod's assistants, who felt almost as rough as Bo', but not quite – worked in suffering silence. Tubbs was in a stinking mood, and Boda wondered if it was to do with his tattoo or the fact he was sort of forced to spend the night in Disgraceland, against his wishes as it were. But Boda soon concluded that the miserable git should have joined in the fun for once, instead of brooding like a big baby and disappearing into the night. He might even have had a bit of action if he'd stayed put. And just as the naked form of Mia, Maya, Milla or whatever her name flashed brightly in his mind's eye, Boda dropped a brick into the boot and sprinted as fast as he could to the nearest shrub to empty his stomach.

Tubbs watched Bo' go, shook his head and placed the last kilo block carefully into the sunken compartment that was built into the boot of the car, before closing the lid and locking it with a small silver key. The pungent aroma disappeared almost at once, thanks to the chest's special lining. Tubbs had the device especially built and installed by an acquaintance of Dutch origin in order to transport his produce up and down the country without having to worry about the stench if he pulled up for a piss somewhere. But just as he was thinking of leaving, Blod appeared – the look on his face more sober than a can of Kaliber.

"How d'it go?" asked Tubbs, which seemed like a very strange question from where Boda was crouching, still dry-heaving into the undergrowth.

"Taken care of. Just as planned."

"Good work," Tubbs answered, a grim look masking his face. "I'll see you next week then." Boda looked on as they hugged each other like old friends, which was a bit weird as he knew that they hadn't even met until yesterday.

Boda spat the last dregs of spittle to the floor and wiped his mouth with the back of his hand. He was glad to see Tubbs getting behind the wheel as well. His wounds must be better today, thought Boda, although to be fair, his friend probably realised that he was in no fit state to drive a golf ball, never mind a motor car.

He joined Tubbs in the Polo and breathed a huge sigh of relief that he was about to escape from Disgraceland without having to face Pennar, but as the car passed the mansion's main entrance, Luca and his entourage appeared waving at Tubbs to stop. Boda's eyes quickly scanned the faces. There was no sign of Pennar among them. He lifted a water bottle off the floor between his feet, took a long swig and lit a cigarette.

"All right, boys?" Luca smiled broadly and shouted his greeting.

"Someone's happy this morning," Tubbs commented while

shaking hands with the rock star, who carried a guitar on his back in a battered case and pulled a small suitcase on wheels behind him.

"It's amazing what an evening in the company of a supermodel can do for you!" retorted Darren, who looked paler than ever hiding behind his Ray-Bans.

"Too right, Dar'. But a bit of kip also helps – as opposed to staying up all night to watch dawn break with Carwyn."

"Yeah, yeah," came the reply, quickly followed by a massive belch.

Beyond Darren stood Sarge and Blim, also hiding behind dark glasses. It was obvious to Tubbs that out of all six of them, only Luca had had any sleep the previous night.

"I thought you were going on tour?" asked Tubbs.

"I *am* going on tour," came Luca's confused reply.

"Where's all your stuff then?"

"Everything's waiting for us out there – Sarge and Blim's equipment, that is. The record company takes care of all that shit. All I need is some clean pants and a guitar. I just hope these fucks are sober enough to remember the songs tomorrow night."

Tubbs heard some mumbling from behind Luca, before the rock god leaned down and stared over his shades at Boda, who looked iller than anyone he'd ever seen.

"Fuckin' hell, Bo! Good night, was it?"

"Too right, Luca. Feeling a bit delicate today though."

"You're not the only one, dude. Same again next month, is it?"

"Fuck yeah. Cheers Luca…"

"No worries. Now drive carefully and take it easy…" And off drove Tubbs, leaving Disgraceland behind, but taking all his worries with him.

As Tubbs aimed the motor eastwards, Boda's self-inflicted

sickness grew worse by the mile. The sweat poured down his face as if his slap-head was the source of a great river, and he was totally convinced that he'd pissed himself although his nethers were dry every time he checked.

Boda stared out the slightly opened side window as the world flashed by, trying to remember what happened last night, even though he didn't *really* want to remember either... just in case. The last thing he recalled was entering the bedroom with Pennar by his side – the pair of them salivating and gurning in equal measures as what's-her-face beckoned them in, her body seemingly glistening in the boudoir's low light. And after that, fuck all. Except for Pennar's naked backside and the look of utter contentment on his still-sleeping face this morning. And as happened every time his inner demons tortured him like this, the biggest ghost of them all was never far behind... and just like that, his father's face appeared in place of Pennar, tearing at his heart and inflaming his hangover a hundredfold.

In an attempt to remove Hawkeye from his head he lit another fag and allowed the music to fill his mind. And as Peter Green's sweet blues soothed the pain somewhat, Boda realised that he and Tubbs hadn't said a word to each other since leaving Disgraceland an hour ago. He pulled hard on the cigarette and turned to look at his friend, wondering what exactly was going through his head at this exact moment in time...

"DS Evans, come on in," T-Bone greeted the older of the two detectives who stood outside his front door in the rain. He'd known DS Evans for many years, but he'd never seen the other one before. He looked fresh somehow. His coat was clean and so was his baby-face. T-Bone didn't like strangers, especially those representing the law.

"This is DC Alban Owen, my new partner," explained the middle-aged dick as they both stepped into the house, dripping water all over the floor.

"Nice to meet you," lied T-Bone as he offered his hand to the young man, before slowly leading them both to his office, limping all the way and leaning heavily on his walking stick. He was lucky to be alive after his accident, but the crash near Libanus had left its mark. On reaching the study, all three sat down. T-Bone hated having to deal with the filth like this, while also realising that there was no way to avoid the inevitable. They were just doing their jobs, after all.

A month had passed since Foxy's funeral and a two since her murder. His left leg was still heavily supported and his ribs were taking forever to heal. His partly-severed ear meant that his head was heavily bandaged and the burns on his neck were slowly scabbing over. The cocktail of drugs he'd been prescribed were easing the pain, no doubt, but they were also messing with his mind. He hadn't seen much of Al since the funeral, but the young buck didn't suspect a thing. Mainly due to the fact that he'd been drunk and high ever since he heard the news.

T-Bone smoothed his moustache, and then asked a question to kickstart the conversation.

"Have you got any news then? Have you found the bastard?"

"Not quite…" started DC Owen, before his senior partner pulled rank.

"From the information we've collected – witness reports and the like – it would appear that the murderer was attempting to impersonate you…"

"According to the reports, he looked just like you – handlebar moustache, long grey hair…"

"But I'm not a suspect?" T-Bone asked while struggling not to laugh in their faces.

"Not at all…"

"You're alibi is completely watertight…"

"*Alibis…*" DS Evans corrected.

"Yes. *Alibis*. We have fifty-plus witnesses who swear you were at the clubhouse on the night in question, so you have no worries there," said DC Owen, although in truth he didn't believe any of the bikers. But unfortunately for the police, without one credible witnesses to what happened at the Safari Inn, they didn't have a hope of building a case against the head Bandido.

"What about the man seen leaving the motel – the one who booked the room?"

"Mr Jones, you mean?"

"Yes. Mr Jones. Although I'd wager that wasn't his real name."

"And me. But we have no leads…"

"And no description either…"

"What about the manager?"

"He can't remember a thing. He's off his tits on anti-depressants according to his wife."

"I'd be fucking depressed too if I worked at the Safari Inn!" said T-Bone, which made all three of them chuckle politely. T-Bone hadn't revealed that his head gardener had disappeared at exactly the same time as the mysterious Mr Jones. The reason for this was twofold – firstly, he didn't know Blod's real name or home address as he paid his workforce with cash; and secondly, he wanted to deal with him personally, the next time their paths crossed… *if* their paths ever crossed again, that is.

"We just wanted to keep you up to date with proceedings…"

With what exactly? T-Bone wanted to ask, as these little piggies hadn't told him anything new. But he bit his tongue in the hope that the porkers would fuck off and leave him alone.

"We'll be in touch if we need you again…"

"Or if something else comes up…"

"Thanks," said T-Bone, although he wasn't sure why, before getting to his feet with the help of his stick and leading them back to the front door safe in the knowledge that the police would never be able to accuse of him of anything now.

He'd been very thorough in covering his tracks. He was back in Rudry before half-eight on the night in question, and had left the car and his clothes burning on Caerphilly common before bombing home on his hog wearing clean garbs and making it to the club by nine, where he appeared in the bar from his office, after getting in through the back door, as if he'd been there all night. In a stroke of luck, the fact that Al was at the clubhouse that night was all-important in the context of a possible case against T-Bone. He was there comforting his friend Boda, as he too drowned his sorrows after losing his father a week or so earlier. Unbeknown to them, T-Bone had played a major role in both their bereavements. And of course, his apparent suicide attempt on his motorbike a few days after the incident supported the accepted theory that he had nothing at all to do with Foxy's death.

On opening the door to let the detectives out, all three heard a voice crackling loudly on the CB radio of the unmarked car parked out front. DC Owen excused himself and ran to the car through the still pouring rain. DS Evans turned to face T-Bone, but didn't say anything until his partner was safely in the driver's seat with the door closed behind him.

"Where did you find this tit?" asked T-Bone, nodding his head towards the car.

"Don't ask! He's a right prat. A bit of an eager beaver, if you know what I mean."

"Does he know?"

"He *suspects*. But he can't prove anything."

"So I'm in the clear?"

"Pretty much. But fuck me T, you were lucky this time. I mean, *really* lucky. All we needed was *one* credible witness. What the fuck came over you to do such a thing?"

T-Bone shrugged. Smiled.

"Don't be so fuckin' cocky. DC Owen by there is desperate for a result. He wants to prove himself, see. First case and all that. And I've had to work very hard to save your ass."

"I appreciate that, you know I do."

"Yeah. Well. I'll be much happier when you pay me for keeping your back by 'ere."

"It's on its way, don't worry. Have I *ever* let you down?"

"Hmmmm," the detective mock-pondered. "And what about that other little problem of yours, have you sorted that yet?"

"Well, Jacques Teamo has now officially left my employment, if you catch my drift."

"I do and I'm glad to hear it. One botched job too many. I mean, I know Hawk had to go after what he did, but snapping his break cables was amateur to say the least. A bloody monkey could have come up with a better plan…"

"A bit too obvious for my liking too. Although no one suspects any foul play…"

"Well that's what happens when you've got friends in high places." Detective Evans smiled proudly. "So you need someone to take his place, am I right?"

"You are."

"Have you got someone in mind?"

"I know the perfect applicant."

"Who?"

"A true blue natural born killer…"

"When will he be ready to start?"

"Soon. I'll let you know."

"I'll be in touch…"

"See you later, Efrog."

"You too. And for fuck's sake don't do anything stupid for a little while. Keep your head down. I need a fuckin' holiday after the month I've had."

After closing the door on the rain and on the rozzers, T-Bone returned to his study and called Al. He had an offer to make him, and although there was no answer in Dinas Powys, T-Bone had a pretty good idea where he could find him.

He grabbed a brolly and shuffled to the golf-cart parked out back, before driving slowly through the rain towards the clubhouse. And that's where he was, sat at the bar with Boda drowning their collective sorrows in a bottle of Wild Turkey, sporting a couple of fresh looking tats on the top of his left arm.

T-Bone knew before reaching the bar that Al would be too drunk to contemplate what he had to offer him this afternoon. In fact the only thing he could think of when he saw his face up close was how much weight the young man had gained since losing his mother. Without wasting a second longer than was necessary in their company, T-Bone arranged for Al to stay the night at the manor house so that they could have a meeting in the morning. Or more likely the following afternoon.

As T-Bone hobbled away from the bar towards his office, he heard Boda call Al 'Tubbs' for the first time. And as he unlocked the door marked 'private', he hoped the nickname wouldn't stick…

Little Al woke up to the unwelcome thud of yet another huge hangover. His parched tongue was licking the carpet of his old bedroom in T-Bone's house, but he had no idea why he was there or how he actually got there. It didn't really matter. Nothing *really* mattered any more. The Foxy-shaped void in his life felt as if it would never be filled. Except on a temporary basis, with a daily dose of hard drinking.

He slowly got to his feet and stumbled to the en-suite, where he filled the sink with cold water and ducked his face right in, causing the fluid to overflow onto the tiled floor and his bare feet. He counted to twenty before coming up for air and that's when he came face-to-face with 'Tubbs' for the first time, staring straight at him from the mirror above the basin. After denying the nickname's appropriateness for a week or so, he suddenly realised that it suited his current appearance perfectly. His cheeks were as chubby as a feasting hamster's while his man-tits, covered as they were right now with a Metallica T-shirt, were crying out for at least a C-cup support. He decided at once that he'd do something about it, before drying himself with a towel and wondering, still half-drunk, towards the kitchen, where he could smell the fresh coffee brewing.

On the landing, he walked past a framed photo of Foxy and T-Bone on holiday in Jamaica a few years ago; then a portrait T-Bone commissioned some artist to paint of his mother in the hall; and lastly, by the kitchen door, a photo of all three of them taken at last year's annual Bandidos' barbecue, all smiles and slightly sunburned.

She was everywhere.

She was nowhere.

On reaching the kitchen, Tubbs went straight for the booze cupboard. He needed something to straighten him out. He needed something to ease the pain. So much so that he didn't even notice T-Bone standing over the oven frying bacon and eggs for his visitor. T-Bone watched him open the cupboard and reach for the bourbon.

"Its *coffee* you need, Al, not booze," he said as calmly and kindly as he could. "Not yet anyway," he added with a wink. "Now sit there, neck these, drink that and eat this…"

And Tubbs did exactly as he was told. He swallowed four strong painkillers with a mouthful of orange juice, sipped some sweet-strong-black coffee and started eating his full English. Slowly.

"Come to the office when you're done," ordered T-Bone, before leaving Al in peace and taking the bottle of bourbon with him, just in case.

Within twenty minutes Al felt much better. Not great. But better than the disabled disaster that woke up an hour or so earlier.

"In," barked T-Bone on hearing the knock on the office door, and once again Al obeyed. He stepped into the large study and came face to face with another picture of his mam, this time staring at him from the wall behind where T-Bone sat.

He sat and stared at the mysterious-looking box that sat on the desk between them.

"That's for you," said T-Bone, nodding towards it.

"What is it?" asked Tubbs, his head starting to throb once again.

"Open it."

He leaned forward, grabbed the dark wooden chest which was carved intricately with Celtic patterns, and pulled it carefully towards him. It was heavy. *Very* heavy. It wasn't big – some fifteen inches by twelve, but it was like lead.

He turned the key in the small copper lock and lifted the lid. His eyes bulged at what he saw. Al looked up at T-Bone and smiled – the exact response the boss was hoping for.

In the box, lying on a red silk handkerchief was a very familiar gun. Al recognised it at once, although he hadn't seen it for more than a decade. Then, slowly, he lifted the .44 Magnum with both hands and examined the hand-cannon's intricate detail.

"It belonged to your mam," T-Bone explained, unnecessarily. "I found it in the drawer by her bed." The lies flowed freely in the knowledge that Little Al suspected nothing.

"Why are you giving it to me?" asked Al, still staring at the steel.

"You need a weapon for two reasons. One, you'll need a gun if you're going to work for me. And two, you need a gun so you can hunt your mother's killer…"

"I don't understand…" Tubbs lowered the gun, carefully placing it back in the box. T-Bone hesitated before answering, considering his response.

"I'm not going to bullshit you, Al, we're too close for any of that. There's an opening in the organisation. An opportunity for you to work for me in a specialised and very lucrative position. I need someone I can trust completely. Someone who has already proved himself in the field, and someone who's been loyal to me down the years…"

"To do *what*?"

"I need an assassin, Al. A hit man. A contract killer. A hired gun. Call it what you like."

Al stared across the table for a good few seconds as T-Bone's words sunk in.

"What are you talking about? I don't get it."

"I know, I know. It's a lot to take in all at once. But let me explain. I've recently had to let someone go, as it were. Long story short, he'd done one botched job too many and that was that. He'd become sloppy. Compromised. I had no choice. I *had* to let him go…" Al understood at once what T-Bone was referring to, and by disclosing this to him, his mentor already had him hooked. Now all he had to do was reel him in and land him.

"But *why* me?" Al's mind was racing. He knew T-Bone was involved in a lot of dodgy dealings, but contract killings were taking things a bit far.

"As I said, I need someone I can trust *completely*, and I also know you've got the killer instinct…"

"What do you mean by *that*?" Al was genuinely confused now, he'd never killed anything bigger that a bunny-rabbit with a BB-gun.

"Come on Al, don't be modest. You're mother told me what you did to Calvin…"

Al stared again, his head pounding and T-Bone's claims confusing him to the core. Back in the Swansea of his childhood, the raised voices woke Little Al from his slumber. He listened carefully to determine whether his mam was there or not, but he couldn't hear any female voices, just four well-oiled idiots arguing in the lounge. He was glad that his bedroom door was locked although, even as a six-year-old, he appreciated that the cheap plywood portal wouldn't offer much protection if any of the hoodlums *really* wanted to come on in. He held his teddy very tightly, snuggled under the duvet and wished that the voices would stop so that he could return to his dreams.

And in the end, Little Al had his wish, but not before the noise reached a crashing crescendo in the form of a deafening *BANG*, followed by hushed whispers, fast-fading footsteps and the front door of the flat closing on the scene of the crime.

Al lay there for a little while, not daring to move or make a noise. He held his breath and waited for sirens that never came. Eventually, he slipped from his bed and leant his ear on the door to listen. Not a peep. So he unlocked the door and stared across the lounge at the sofa. The television was on, broadcasting a heavy snowstorm of utter irrelevance and casting evil shadows over Calvin's headless corpse. Al could see the blackness splashed over the wall behind him, and the gun which lay on the floor by his feet.

Little Al tiptoed towards his father, his eyes wide with fear and relief. He grabbed the gun and ran back to bed, locking the door behind him. And the next thing he remembered was Foxy shaking him awake, a smile dancing on her beautiful face, her eyes filled with dreams of freedom.

"I *know* you can do this job for me," T-Bone's voice sliced through his subconscious, bringing him back to the here and now.

"But… I don't want to… you know…"

"I've never asked you for anything, have I? And I *really* need your help by here…" Al felt a pang of guilt at the reminder of his debt to the only loved one he had left. "I'm too old to do it myself, and…" T-Bone paused for full effect.

"And what?" Al bit the bait.

"Well… you're like a son to me, Al. No… correction… you *are* my son. I need your help and considering where I found you and your mother all those years ago…" he didn't finish the sentence. He didn't need to.

"But… *killing*… *murdering*…" Al shook his head, which had miraculously stopped pounding for the time being, and T-Bone could see that he was slowly coming round.

"*Criminals*, Al. *Hoods. Scum.* Call them what you will. Not to mention helping your old man and earning tens of thousands of pounds…" That got his full attention.

"How much?"

"Twenty grand to be exact."

"A year?"

"Per job." Al swallowed hard as T-Bone continued. "At least three a year. No more than six. Which equals sixty grand, guaranteed. Tax-free of course," T-Bone added with a grin. "Better than the alternative, I'm sure you'd agree."

"But what if I get caught?"

"You *won't* get caught. And even if you do, you'll be protected at all times. I have friends in very high places, Al. Only you and I will know about our agreement. No one else. You'll receive two months' intensive training before the first job. You'll be like a ninja by that time. I've got contacts in the police force. *Allies* as opposed to *friends*, but allies that appreciate the service I provide. Around eighty percent of the work comes directly through the force. You'll be above the law…"

"I don't know… that sounds a bit too good to be true."

"I know it sounds far-fetched, but what can I say? – it's the truth. And it won't be forever anyway, if you ever find the bastard who killed your mother, you can walk away, no questions asked." T-Bone looked into his eyes as he said this. "You've *got* to trust me, Al."

"But…"

"Do you trust me, Al?"

"Of course," was his answer.

The wrong answer.

"I got to go 'n see T-Bone," stated Tubbs, disturbing the silence as the Polo glided past junction 33 of the M4 and the turn-off for Cardiff Bay, Penarth and Dinas Powys beyond.

"Whatever," came Boda's reply, who until that point had been floating in and out of a trance since they passed the signs to Swansea.

Although Tubbs *did* believe what Blod had told him, he still didn't *want* to believe him, and had to give T-Bone another chance somehow. A chance to do what exactly, he didn't know. He had no idea why he was going to see him either, but somehow needed to look him in the eyes and test the old bastard a little, to see how many lies, if any, he'd feed him today.

Tubbs realised now that he and his mother had paid a very high price for their debt to T-Bone, while also concluding that the head-Bandido had also made him, *forced* him, to be what he had become.

Tubbs pulled up outside the clubhouse and left Boda asleep

in the car, but on entering the bar he was informed by Jess, the barmaid, that the boss had headed home for lunch, so back he went to the motor before driving up the well-hidden dirt track towards his old home.

Once more, Tubbs left his friend quietly snoring as *In The Sky* kicked in on the CD player for the third time that morning, and made for the back door of the manor house, which he opened with his key.

Tubbs hadn't visited T-Bone's home for a month or so and neither had the cleaners, by all accounts. T-Bone was too old to look after the place himself, and even in his youth would never have considered getting the vacuum cleaner out or giving the place a quick dusting. The kitchen floor was sticky, while the carpet that covered the stairs was dirty and worn. The bins needed emptying, but he wasn't going to do anything to help the old man. Not now. Not anymore.

Across the hall, Tubbs could hear voices coming from the office, but as he tiptoed nearer, he realised that T-Bone was listening to Five Live, as opposed to talking business with an associate.

His heart pounded as he knocked the door.

"In," came the command, and that's exactly what Tubbs did, and came face to face with the man who murdered his mother – the man he'd been searching for all his adult life. "Al, Al, Al," beamed T-Bone, before shuffling around the desk and bear-hugging his old apprentice.

Tubbs saw through the deceit for the very first time. The facade had collapsed completely now, leaving nothing but a dead man standing before him.

After wading through the usual chit-chat, Tubbs asked: "What you doing next Friday? I've got a couple of tickets to the Monster Jam at the Millennium Stadium and was wondering if you wanted to come. You know, like old times…"

Tubbs saw T-Bone hesitate before answering, as his mind searched for an acceptable answer.

"Next Friday?" he began, before digging deeper for a reason. T-Bone reached for his diary and opened it, making a show of looking at the date in question. He shook his head, looked disappointed. "Sorry Al, I've got a meeting planned with Big Don Chambers, you know, the head of the Birmingham Outlaws. We've got some business to discuss. I've already cancelled once, so I can't pull out this time," he explained weakly.

Tubbs nodded his understanding, while marvelling at the lameness of the excuse. He wanted to grab the diary and expose the lie, but now wasn't the time or the place. He'd wait a week, no worries.

The old friends bullshitted for a few minutes more, before Tubbs turned his back and returned to the car with his heart shattered and his mind in a right mess. While walking towards the car and the sleeping tattooist within, he wondered if he was any better than T-Bone, considering that he'd also kept a dark secret from his best friend for more than a decade. As he opened the door and squeezed in behind the wheel, he decided that he had to tell Boda the truth at the first opportunity that came his way.

CROSSING PATHS

"**D**AH BANDULU be back, aye be sure ah dat," Vexl stated, as the opening titles to *Crossroads* filled the lounge.

"I knows," Vicky agreed, although she wasn't certain. "That's wot he said innit."

"Nah tuh get *yah*, pum-pum. Back fuh good. Back wheh he belong."

"Oh," said Vicky, completely confused, as she tried to decipher exactly what Vexl had said, while Richard Gere and Gary Barlow, for some reason, popped into her head singing a horrible duet. She shook her head to straighten it out, and turned her attention to the half-smoked spliff she held in her hand.

After Gimp had fled that morning, Vicky washed and dressed Vexl's wounds through a combination of pity and fear. As she went to work it soon became clear that he needed some proper medical attention, especially for the deep gash in his shoulder, but Vexl wouldn't have any of it. He hated hospitals, so he said. But he hated every*thing* and every*one*, so what hope for the NHS?

Vexl hadn't harmed her physically since Gimp had left, yet the psychological damage he'd done to her over the years was enough to stop her from exacting any revenge, even if he was at her mercy for a short time as she cleaned the gaping hole at the top of his arm. Vicky had seen what the pimp could do to those who crossed him, and she was very worried about what he'd do to Gimp when he returned to get her. *If* he'd return, that is.

After a pretty hideous life, her heart was already preparing for the worst. Of course, she *wanted* Gimp to come for her, to rescue her, while at the same time she didn't expect it. That's what life had done to her – left her dreading every outcome, as she'd never come close to anything resembling a happy ending.

Vicky sparked up and melted into the sofa. She held the spliff for Vexl to take it, but he was already in another dimension and didn't notice, so she took one last blast, stood up and placed the joint between his fingers.

There was a knock at the door and despite his apparent lethargy, Vexl was up in an instant to answer it. If it was Gimp, he didn't want Vicky getting there first, as he didn't trust her. In fact, he didn't trust anyone anymore.

Vicky's heart was racing in anticipation, but it slowed to a canter on hearing a stranger's voice at the brothel's entrance.

"Skin yuh teeth girly, yuh gots yuhsel some c'mpnee," said Vexl on his return, before ushering Vicky towards the stairs.

Leaning on the wall in the hallway was a man who'd obviously already had a skinful, although it wasn't yet mid-afternoon. He had a stupid grin on his face, a badly executed comb-over on his dome and a full-wood in his tight polyester slacks. Vicky felt sick at the sight of him, but knew that there was no avoiding the inevitable, so she went up to her bedroom as Vexl demanded payment up front. The drunk soon joined her and while they tossed, turned and fucked without any feeling, she only had one thing, one man, on her mind.

The sun felt so good as it massaged Petra's skin while she lazed in the secret garden with a toothless cat for company. He probably didn't get much attention, she guessed, as he would 'purrrrrrrr' like a newly-serviced Porsche every time she'd stroke him. She'd decided to stay there for a little while, just in case Vexl and Gimp were out looking for her. They'd never find her here, and she'd make her way to Cardiff after dark. In the meantime, she'd finished reading her novel, then proceeded to pick some super sticky buds and combined the collie with a Marlboro Light to create a mellow high that was still lingering.

Her belly groaned with hunger, so she headed to the greenhouse that housed the tomatoes and picked a handful to keep the pangs at bay, although she knew she'd have to eat something more substantial pretty soon. Then she lay down again on the soft grass, gave the cat some love and let her mind wonder. As always, her parents would pay her a visit, and to follow, a feeling of absolute emptiness. It hit her then just how lonely she was. She had no one. She had nothing. She was all alone. She stared to cry…

When Tubbs killed the engine, Boda opened his eyes and saw that they were back in Dinas Powys. His head was still pounding and his tongue was drier than a Bedouin's back-pack, so he headed for the nearest crib.

"Bed," he mumbled over his shoulder.

"What about our session?" asked Tubbs.

"Later," waved the tattooist, although he was amazed that Tubbs was ready to go again. That boy's pain threshold was gargantuan, fair play. He reached the cabin and realised that the door was locked, so he placed his forehead against the cold glass, closed his eyes and waited for Tubbs to bring the key, which he did in a few minutes as he hauled the chest from the car that contained the ten kilos of cannabis, carrying it effortlessly, biceps bulging under the weight.

"Open the door for us, would you Bo'? If you can manage it…" asked Tubbs still holding the chest aloft, so Boda turned around, grabbed the keys from his pocket and unlocked the door, before heading straight for the spare bed, leaving Tubbs to it. As he watched his best friend bolt for the bedroom, Tubbs pondered how he could ever tell him the truth about his father after all these years, without ending their otherwise rock-solid relationship. But in truth it didn't matter, as Tubbs had no choice now. He *had* to tell him. He had to do the right thing. Otherwise he was no better than T-Bone.

Brick-by-brick, Tubbs took the ganja to the bathroom, where he hid it in the well-insulated and watertight compartment underneath the intricately tiled floor. Then he got undressed and stepped into the shower, taking care to wash his wounded leg and the rest of his tired, heavily-tattooed husk. As the water flowed over his head and shoulders, he closed his eyes and opened his mind. The last twenty-four hours had well and truly turned his world upside down. T-Bone's lies echoed between his ears. The old man deserved all that was coming his way.

He shaved, washed and had a wank; before drying, dressing, feeding the cats and going to see how Victor was doing today. Miserable and moping around the place, as usual, he guessed…

Gimp quietly closed the garden gate behind him and followed the pristine path past all sorts of flowers and shrubs towards the front door. Colourful baskets hung on both sides of the entrance, recently watered by the look of the wet patches on the floor beneath them. He rang the bell and waited a while before a form appeared on the other side of the frosted glass door.

Gimp hadn't come far. He didn't need to. He'd get his hands on exactly what he needed right here, in Sully, a stone's throw from the Captain's Wife.

"Password?" the blur asked.

"Password?" replied Gimp. He hadn't been here for many years, but couldn't recall ever being asked for a password before. He had hoped that Clinton would have remembered him, after all he was quite a memorable sort, but now he was just worried that he'd wasted his time coming here at all.

"*Password.*"

"Wot password? Vere's neva been a password."

"Of course there has. How else am I supposed to separate the good guys from the boys in blue?"

"I dunno mate. If vey wearin' a uniform, dahnt let ve fuckers in?"

"Very good, very good," the Eton-accented voice conceded. "But not good enough…"

"Do I look like a fackin coppa to you?" asked Gimp, his patience being tested.

"As a matter of fact, you do. A short one, for sure, but you smell like a swine and your eyes are shiftier than a well-oiled gearstick. Now what's the password you short-arsed bugger?"

And that's when Gimp realised that not only did Clinton remember him, but that he was also ripping the piss.

"Clinton yuh fukka! You ad me goin vere, ya cunt!"

"I know old boy, but I couldn't resist when I saw your ugly mug on the CCTV," Clinton said on opening the door, the smile on his face reflecting Gimp's. "Long time no nothing…"

He hadn't changed at all, and apart from a few white hairs on his head he looked exactly as he did the last time Gimp had seen him, some three years ago. He was in his forties now – a handsome man from a wealthy background. After losing his mother as a young man, Clinton had been raised by his father, who happened to be an international arms dealer, and more nannies than he cared to remember. When his father passed away during a business trip to Angola in 1989, Clinton inherited the business but decided to take it down a different route and concentrate on the local market, using his father's old contacts to offer the south Wales underworld some of the best weapons on the black market.

Gimp followed him through the huge hallway to the colossal kitchen. Clinton lived alone and kept his business dealings close to his chest, as he had to in his line of work. His home was a façade of domesticity; beautifully decorated throughout with a couple of original and expensive canvasses hanging here and there. That's not to say it was showy; if anything, it was understated. Like many other wealthy men, golf was his only hobby. Not very original, granted, but a good way to waste his days as the money poured in to his offshore accounts.

Clinton fixed them both a G&T, as Gimp got straight to the point.

"I need a shoota, Clint."

"Really? And here I was thinking that this was a social call…"

"Sorry," Gimp said, feeling a bit silly.

"Don't be soft, dear boy, I'm only fucking with you, to use the profane parlance of our times. It's good to see you, but come on, business *is* business…"

"Too true. Anyway…"

"What do you need a gun for Gimp, nothing to do with that scar on your face is it? I hope you're not planning anything too extreme?" Gimp lifted his hand to his face, but ignored Clinton's question.

"*Protection*, Clint. Naffin more. I'm leavin tahn, an takin my laydee wiv me. Only problem is she belongs to someone else..."

As he approached the greenhouses at the bottom of his garden, Tubbs froze to the spot when he saw her. At first, he took her for an apparition, his mother's ghost, lying with Victor by the palm tree; Foxy's final resting place. But, as he stared hard through the rhododendron, he noticed one obvious difference – the fresh-looking scar on her cheek – that told him it wasn't Foxy's spirit.

He continued to stare for a good few minutes, his heart racing and the palms of his hands sweating, before deciding that he had to approach her, he had to say hello. He started walking casually towards her, and did a really naff double-take when he stepped around the corner, pretending to see her for the first time. She was very young, no older than twenty, but she was so similar to his mother that Tubbs really didn't know how to react...

Petra froze when she saw the giant walking towards her. Then she sat up with a start, causing Victor – who was fast asleep on her breast and belly – to scarper towards a nearby butterfly bush.

The first thing that sprang to her mind was that he must work for Vexl and that he'd somehow tracked her down and was now going to force her to return to the brothel in Barry. But after thinking about it for just a second, she concluded correctly that it made no sense at all. Then she remembered that she was in fact trespassing on private property and that the best thing for everyone would be to leave. At once.

She got to her feet and looked in his direction. Their eyes met. He was huge, no doubt, and also seemed a little ungainly, as most large men tended to. After her performance in outfoxing Vexl this morning, she was confident that she could side-step her way past this Goliath as well.

The way he looked at her made her very uneasy – as if he was staring right through her and into her soul. His kind and clean-shaved cherubic face didn't quite match his heavily tattooed hulk either, which were on show on his bare arms and legs, thanks to his black vest and combat shorts combo. Petra loved tats. But now wasn't the time to develop a crush.

She looked around for the best escape route, but then remembered her case. *Shit!* was the next thing that came to her mind. Followed by *Fuck it!* And she was off, leaving her belongings behind and making a break for the left-hand path. She disappeared into the dense undergrowth without looking back.

Tubbs shook his head and smiled on seeing the trail she chose, before taking a couple of steps to his left and the other entrance/exit to the exact same path. He waited there, still smiling, and right on cue she came running towards him, and that's when he grabbed her in his arms and held her tightly until she stopped wriggling and screaming.

Initially she was like an eel as she tried everything to escape his hold, but she had no hope and soon realised this and stopped squirming.

"You forgot your suitcase," Tubbs said, his soft voice taking her by surprise, while not fully erasing her fears.

"Don't take me back there!" Petra pleaded. "Don't hurt me. *Please* don't hurt me!"

"Back where?" Tubbs asked, completely lost. "And why would I want to hurt you?"

Gently, Tubbs placed her feet on the floor, but didn't let go of her arms. He half-expected her to try and escape once again, but she stood there paralysed with fear. He looked at her face and couldn't believe the way it echoed Foxy's.

Petra was breathing heavily in an attempt to control the adrenalin coursing through her body. She decided not to reveal any more to this strange man, just in case he was trying to trick her.

"You can ler go now," Petra said. "I'm not gonna run…"

"You don't seem to know the way out anyway," Tubbs smiled.

Petra sat cross-legged on the floor and reached for her fags. She lit one and inhaled deeply, before offering the stranger one.

"No thanks. I don't smoke," he said, taking a seat – in the lotus position – on the floor by her side. His wounded knee made him wince, but Tubbs managed to suppress the pain somehow.

"You liah!" Petra exclaimed. "I've seen what's in your greenhouse!"

"Ok. I don't smoke *cigarettes* then."

"Good. Theyah very bad for you," Petra said, toking hard on the one in her hand. Tubbs smiled. Petra did the same.

Was she flirting with him? It had been so long since Tubbs had spent any time with a woman, that he didn't have a clue. But whatever she was doing, he liked it.

Victor joined them, rubbing his chin on Petra's legs and purring in ecstasy. Tubbs couldn't believe the way he was behaving. He hadn't been so friendly since...

"Welcome back, Victor," Tubbs said, stroking his head before moving down his back and making his tail dance like a cobra in a market in Marrakech.

"Where's he been?" asked Petra. This huge man and his gentle nature had already effortlessly won her over. For some reason, she wanted to know everything about him. Right now.

"Nowhere, I just haven't seen him so happy since..." Tubbs's sentence tailed off. But Petra innocently wanted an answer.

"Since when?"

"Since Mam died," explained Tubbs, which compelled Petra to reach across and gently hold his spade-like hand. Tubbs looked up at her and saw that she was staring intensely back at him.

Petra's earlier concerns had disappeared almost entirely by now. She saw beyond the tattoos and the gruff exterior, and melted in the honeypot that was his nature. No man had ever truly touched her heart before. Plenty had tried, of course, but they never usually got past her nipples. Her first instinct was to always raise her defences and block all incoming emotional missiles. She found it easy to switch off, and although she wasn't sure what that said about her, right now, she didn't care. All she knew was that sitting here with this stranger, she suddenly felt safe, and had no intention of flicking the off switch. She also felt slightly horny, although that would have to wait.

Tubbs on the other hand had stumbled across all his dreams wrapped up in one tidy little package. He squeezed her hand and smiled.

"Petra," she said, snapping Tubbs out of his daydreams.

"What?"

"My name. Petra. And you are?"

"Al. But everyone calls me Tubbs."

"Well I'm going to call you Al, ok?"

Tubbs nodded as his heart skipped a beat, and then Petra's stomach piped up and declared its hunger with a low growl that made Victor stop and stare for a second or two in its direction.

"Come on," Tubbs said, getting to his feet and offering Petra his hand so that she could do the same, before grabbing her case and leading his new lady-friend towards his log cabin.

After a bowl each of homemade leek and potato soup and some bread from the local bakehouse, Tubbs offered to wash her wound. Luckily for Petra, it wasn't very deep, although Tubbs guessed that it would leave a small scar for sometime, possibly forever.

Who did this to her and why? Tubbs wondered, although he didn't want to ask. *And how did she end up in his garden?* He remembered the fear that gripped her when he first approached her, but *what* was she scared of, or more to the point – *who*? He decided not to ask her yet. He hoped that she'd stay with him for a while, and would maybe confide in him later on.

"I've never met anyone called Petra before, were you conceived in Jordan or something?" Tubbs asked, while applying the TCP.

"What? Where?"

"Were you conceived in Jordan?"

"What sorta question is that? I don't get it."

"Well, Petra's a famous archaeological site in Jordan. Haven't you seen *Indiana Jones and the Last Crusade*? The climax was filmed in Petra, you know, where Indy found the Grail before riding off into the sunset…"

"So?"

"Well, sometimes people name their children after where the child was conceived. Brooklyn Beckham for example, and Jonathan Ross-on-Wye…"

"Oh. Ok. I understand now," she said, without taking any notice of his terrible joke. "But I don't think my pares eva went to Jordan. The people of the Gurnos don't get much furtha than Asda, down Murtha. Ponty at a stretch. And anyway, I was named afta the Blue Peter dog."

Boda leaned on the doorframe, watching Tubbs and the pretty girl interact with each other through the thick fog of his lingering hangover. She looked familiar for some reason, while his best friend's good mood was completely alien.

He recalled Tubbs's dark disposition on the journey home from Disgraceland and was amazed at the transformation. A wide smile seemed to have been pasted onto his usually scowling face. *What the fuck was going on?* But the answer was obvious after thinking about it. Boda sparked the half-smoked spliff that he didn't manage to finish before passing out in the spare room, and Tubbs and the girl turned to look in his direction.

"How long have I been out for?" asked Boda through the purple haze and half-closed eyes.

"A few hours," answered Tubbs. "Why?"

"Well, I was just wondering where and how you managed to find this beautiful creature in such a short period of time." Tubbs looked at the 'creature' and smiled as he saw her cheeks flush.

"I found her in the greenhouse," answered Tubbs, before Petra and he laughed at the absurdity of the truth. Boda stared at them and shook his head. Although he was totally lost – thanks to the hangover, the green and the ridiculousness of the answer – he was well happy to see his best friend smiling. Not to mention the fact that it looked as if Tubbs was on the verge of pulling and possibly getting laid. He stepped to the kettle and handed the joint to the girl, noticing the scar as he did so – the only flaw to her near perfection.

"I'm Boda," he said, offering her his hand to shake.

"Petra."

"What happened to your face? That scar looks fresh," Boda asked the question that Tubbs was dying to, which caused Petra's whole body to tighten. She didn't want to reveal the truth about what she was doing for a living less than twenty-four hours ago, so she decided to lie. Why change a habit of a lifetime?

"You ok?" Tubbs asked, sensing her discomfort. He reached out and took her hand gently in his, and that's when Petra changed her mind and decided that it was time for a proper new beginning. No half-measures. Not now she'd found her man. After a lifetime of lying through her teeth, she was ready to trust someone and open her heart completely.

"Yes. I am. Thanks, Al. But I don't know where to start really…"

"Well, take your time and you can tell us both as I work on Tubbs's leg," Boda suggested, before heading for the lounge where his equipment was waiting for him following the previous day's session.

"What sorta *work*?" Petra asked, before Tubbs led her by the hand to the lounge and rolled up the right leg of his three-quarter length combat shorts where the intricate dragon awaited the needle once again.

Petra sat on a bulging bean-bag near the stereo, stroking Victor – who was still following her everywhere – watching the scene with some interest. Al was recumbent on the Lazyboy, while Boda went to work on the huge tattoo that ran the full length of his right leg. She looked at Al, who seemed to be in a trance. When she saw him first, she thought that he was a bit fat. Chubby. Chunky. Along those lines anyway. Definitely a little overweight at least. But now, with his skin tensed and pulled tight in response to the needle's incessant scribbling, Petra could see that his muscular shell was like a suit of armour protecting his skeleton. He was as still as a sculpture and Petra couldn't take her eyes off him.

"Ready when you are," Boda said, without looking up from his work.

"Ok. Here goes. Right... Yesterday morning I was kidnapped..." and off she went, without stopping once, to regale them with her story. She explained her background and the part she played in her parents' death, the need to escape, her hopes and dreams and the way they were almost extinguished by Vexl. She told them everything about her time in Barry – well, *almost* everything – including the way Vexl treated Gimp and Vicky, the drug-abuse, the knives and finally the climactic fight in the front garden. "He carries at least four knives," she concluded. "Possibly more. Including one huge blade unda his armpit. He's gotta real fetish, I reckon..."

Boda turned to face her at this point, nodded, but returned to Tubbs's leg without uttering a word.

"Anyway, I can't rememba everythen, adrenalin I suppose, but he was kneelen above me on the garden path and the next thing I know he's got a cut-throat razor in his hand and that's when I pretended to pass out. He started sayen somethen then..."

Petra imitated her captor. Badly. "I'm gonnah scah yah widda lettah vee, so everee time yah see yah reflection in dah mirrah, windah or a back ah spoon, you'll t'ink ah me..."

"What sort of accent is that supposed to be?" asked Boda, his back still turned.

"Jamaican, although he comes from Birmingham according to Vicky, so fuck knows why he speaks like 'at. He's nor even black..."

"He sounds like a proper twat," said Boda, and Petra didn't disagree.

She continued with the story – her escape from Vexl's clutches, her long walk to freedom and finding sanctuary in Al's garden, but when she reached the end, she was met with nothing but silence, except for the needle's eternal whine. Petra lit a cigarette and hoped that Al could forgive her, although the long silence didn't fill her with confidence.

The needle fell silent as Boda finished his work for the day. Tubbs opened his eyes and looked straight at Petra with a very serious look on his face. Her heart shattered into a million little pieces, but Al soon put them all back together again.

"Do you believe in fate, Petra?" he asked, as the warm smile returned.

"Yes!" Petra exclaimed in relief.

"So do I," Tubbs concurred, as the smile disappeared once again. He slowly got to his feet, just as Boda finished applying the Preparation H to his leg. "C'mon Bo', let's pay this Vexl character a visit. I want to have a little chat with him about his conduct…"

"Sweet!" Boda's hangover had lifted completely now, as he tried to remember the last time he saw his friend act so impulsively. Not since before mother's death, was his conclusion. Was he witnessing the rebirth of Tubbs, or the last act of a desperately lonely man? "What have you got in mind?" he asked, as he packed up his equipment and headed for the door.

"An eye for an eye. A scar for a scar."

"Be careful," Petra pleaded like the lead actress in a hammed-up Hollywood melodrama. "He's off his 'ead and doesn't care about anythen."

"I fucking hate nihilists," retorted Boda, while Tubbs turned to face her and looked down into her deep blue eyes.

Her recent travails didn't seem to worry him at all, Petra was glad to notice. *Was his past even darker than hers?* If so, she'd be more than happy to heal his wounds. Behind his unexpected gentleness, Petra sensed some serious grief, and all of a sudden she wasn't worried at all about his and Boda's safety.

"We'll be back in an hour or so. Two tops. Now what's the address?"

"Shit! I don't even know the name of the street, but it's the one ova-looken the funfair. Numbah thirteen."

"Anything else we should know?"

"There'll be three of them there – Vexl, Gimp and Vicky. Possibly four if she's gorra client. Oh yeah, it's the second left after the Safari Inn…"

Tubbs shivered on hearing the name. He wasn't expecting that and he closed his eyes and breathed deeply. He felt Petra's hand caress his face. He'd never fully get over the loss, of course, but he definitely felt some new hope today.

"What have you got lined up then?" asked Boda, as he drove the van slowly past Dow Corning as night fell fast.

"I don't know," admitted Tubbs, as his true nature reasserted itself and smothered his earlier thirst for retribution.

"*What?*"

"What can I say, Bo'? I have no idea what I'm going to do when I get there. I mean, I know he deserves a kick-in at the very least, but really now, I don't know…"

Boda laughed. "Fuckin' hell, Tubbs, you're off your head! What was all that bravado back there just now then?"

"Exactly that. Bravado. I don't know what came over me…"

"I do." said Boda, and turned to look at his passenger. But Tubbs didn't ask for a further explanation. He didn't want to hear it. He didn't care. But Boda wasn't to know that, and so he said: "You know who she reminds me of, don't you?"

"Yes," was Tubbs's curt answer, which helped Boda realise that his friend saw the similarity as a positive, as opposed to a confusing and fucked-up factor.

"What now then?" He changed the subject. "Drive round like a couple of teenagers? Supper at Maccy Dees? A pint in the Star?"

Tubbs shrugged his huge shoulders. "What d'you reckon?"

"Well…" Boda smiled. "I've got a bit of an idea…"

They found the street and found the house, before watching the place for a good ten minutes. They saw one man leave and another enter; as well as the dreadlocked freak who answered the door.

"Let's do this," Boda finally ran out of patience and retrieved his equipment from the back of the van. Tubbs followed slowly, his leg tearing and bleeding with every move he made. "You take this," demanded Boda, handing the big man a rusty machete.

"Why?"

"Fuck me Tubbs! Just give this Vexl a good whack and I'll do the rest, ok."

"I'm not going to stab anyone!"

"Did I say *stab*? Did I? No I fucking didn't. Twat him. Whack him. Slap him. Hit him. I don't care what you do, as long as he's unconscious when you've finished with him, ok?"

"Alright, Bo', calm down," Tubbs agreed, before taking the lead and limping towards the brothel.

Boda knocked the door and stepped back. Tubbs stood right behind him, looking hard, while holding the machete behind his back.

The door opened and Vexl stood there as his drug-addled mind slowly evaluated the situation.

"Cyan aye hyelp yah bad bwoyz?" he asked, as Boda and Tubbs did their best not to laugh at his ridiculous accent.

"We're looking for Petra," Boda began. "Is she here?"

"Nyah, thyat craven dundus cold I up dis mwornin."

"She left, is that what you mean?"

"Yah mon, she did wan dis morn…"

"We know," Tubbs joined in. "That's why we're here…"

Vexl stared at them for a while as Tubbs's words hit their mark, before stepping back and attempting to close the door. Unfortunately for him, Boda had foreseen this course of action and had placed one of his size elevens in the doorway to stop Vexl from locking them out, and when the door sprang back towards him, Vexl instinctively reached for the knife under his armpit. Unlike this morning, it didn't catch, and he held it up for all to see in the hope that it would be enough of a deterrent. However, that wasn't quite the case.

"*Wwwwwww*," went Boda, like Les Dennis impersonating Mavis Riley. "He's got a knife!" Vexl froze in utter confusion. Things didn't bode well, somehow…

"*That's not* a knife," Tubbs said in a really bad Australian accent, and after Boda had stepped out the way, Tubbs pulled the blade from behind his back and pointed in the direction of the dread. "*This* is a knife," he cracked the punchline, and followed it up with a swift and severe right hand punch that caught the pimp between his left eye and ear, sending him crashing to the floor in a heap of pain. Then, Tubbs kicked him in the head as T-Bone's face flashed before him, and continued to stomp until Boda pulled him off.

"What's the matter with you, man?" Boda bellowed. "Fuck's sake, I'll have to clean him up now. Nice one, Tubbs. Grab his legs, would you."

The big man mumbled an apology before they lifted the dread by the arms and feet and carried him into the empty lounge.

"What now?" asked Tubbs, although he could have taken a guess.

"Tie him up, arms and legs like," replied Boda, preparing the needle and ink for an impromptu session.

"What was that?" They both stopped and listened for a second as the headboard upstairs banged repeatedly against the wall.

"Shall I go and say hello?" asked Tubbs, with a sly smile.

"It'd be rude not to," answered Boda, as he turned his attention to the dozing dread lying on the sofa.

Tubbs left him to it and, machete in hand, made his way to the source of the knocking. He paused outside the door and listened.

Knock-knock-knock, went the headboard.

Uh-uh-uh, went the customer.

The prostitute, however, didn't make a sound.

Tubbs opened the door and came face-to-face with the whitest pair of ass-cheeks he'd ever seen – real or imaginary – pumping a haggard-looking skeleton, who lay there dead-eyed and dead bored. The prossie looked at him silently for a second, then screamed at the top of her lungs and pushed the punter out of and off her, causing him to fall to the floor on all fours. On seeing Tubbs, the punter stood and pulled up his pants while the hooker cowered in the corner of the room.

"Sorry to disturb you," said Tubbs politely, as the man pushed past him complaining about the fact that he didn't get to shoot his load. Tubbs watched him go just to make sure he left without disturbing Boda downstairs, and when the front door closed, he turned and smiled at the whore. "Vicky? It is Vicky, right?" Her eyes widened but she didn't answer. "Sorry about the disturbance but we've just come to see Vexl. Business. You know how it is. Give us half-an-hour and we'll be out of your hair. Sit tight and don't panic alright, we'll be gone in a jiffy…"

Tubbs left her where she was and locked the door from the outside to make sure she didn't do anything silly, before he rejoined Boda in the lounge. The noise of the needle made his whole leg throb, so he sat and watched and rubbed Preparation H on his wound.

"What d'you think?" asked the tattooist, as he finished off his latest masterpiece.

"Very cruel," Tubbs smiled.

Before leaving, Boda grabbed the Polaroid camera from his bag – the one he used to record the end of each job. "A gift for Petra," he said, before snapping away. And as Boda packed up his gear, Tubbs went back upstairs to unlock Vicky's door before they left.

Vicky listened to them laughing but she had no idea what was going on. Vexl didn't seem to say a word, not that she could hear anyway. Whatever was going on down there, she hoped they fucked him up good and proper. He deserved whatever he got. The hulk that disturbed her last customer looked pretty tasty, especially with the machete, and even after her bedroom door was unlocked and the strangers had left, she stayed where she was in the corner, just in case.

Within a few minutes, the front door opened again. *They must have forgotten something*, she thought, reaching for her L&Bs.

"Vicky!" She heard her name being called, but at first didn't recognise the voice. "Where a'ya dollface?"

She sprang to her feet and opened the door.

"Gimp! I thought you'd neva come!"

"Come dahn ere luv, you gotsta see vis…"

She ran down stairs and found Gimp standing in the lounge, gun in hand, staring at Vexl's body, which lay motionless on the sofa. Vicky and Gimp kissed and had a bit of a cuddle, before turning their attention once more to the pimp.

"Who ve fack did vis, it wozn't you, woz it?"

"Nuh, I dunnow who they were but they only left a few minutes ago."

"It's too much innit, I can't stop larffin at ve poor cunt!"

"Is it for real?" Vicky asked, struggling to believe her eyes.

"Vats wot I fought to start wiv, but look, the ink's fresh as fuck and vere's a bit of blood on his upper lip."

Vicky stepped to Vexl and took a closer look at his new permanently-etched moustache, which lay somewhere between Salvador Dali and General Melchett and made the ridiculous Rasta look even more freakish than before. Although in truth, the tash was nothing compared to the crude cock and balls that were etched on his forehead.

"You ready to go?" asked Gimp, suddenly on edge.

"All packed. I didn't think you'd come for me. I'll just get my stuff…" and off she went up the stairs again, where she collected her bags and some money she'd been hiding, before returning to the lounge and finding Gimp standing on the back of the sofa, carefully removing the *Scream* print from its position on the wall.

"Pass us his keys, dollface," Gimp ordered, when he saw her standing there. Vicky crouched down, quickly searched Vexl and found them in his trouser pocket.

"Wotcha doin?"

"Just takin' wots mine dahlin… wots *ahs* I mean," and that's when Vicky saw the safe deposit box hidden behind the picture. Not the most original place to put one, granted, but Vicky had never known of its existence until today, and she'd lived here as long as Vexl and Gimp had.

Gimp unlocked the safe and emptied its contents into a gaping rucksack he held in one hand. Vicky had never seen so much cash – piles and piles, all neatly stacked and held together with rubber bands. After emptying the safe, Gimp zipped the bag and jumped to the ground.

"Wel, me ol' mucka," he turned to Vexl. "Vis is it. Can't say it's been a pleasure…" before kicking him square in the nuts and hissing: "I ain't yuh bitch no more," under his breath, and pocketing the car keys. "Cam on dahlin, let's get aht o' ere."

"I'll be there now. I forgot summin upstairs," Vicky lied as she watched Gimp leave the house and make his way to the car, which was parked out front. When he was safely sat behind the wheel, she turned to look at her pimp and pulled a syringe from her coat pocket. "I've got a little something for you, Vex," she sang, and leaned down towards him. "A goodbye gift if you like. I've wanted to give it to you for a long long time." The barrel of the syringe held a reddish liquid – Vicky's infected blood. She looked at the moustachioed muppet lying before her as the memories of her time in his stable rushed through her mind in fast-forward.

One of Vexl's eyes fluttered open, and he managed to mumble something unintelligible. His eyes closed again, and that's when Vicky pushed the needle into a prominent vein on his turkey neck and watched as her blood left the syringe and entered his body…

"Safe if I drop you off here?" asked Boda as they approached the top of Tubbs's street.

"Don't you want to come in for a drink or a smoke or something?"

"Come off it, dude. Two's company, three's a gooseberry an' all that…"

"Cheers, Bo'. For everything," Tubbs said as the friends shook hands on a job well done. Behind his smile, however, the shame and repulsion still simmered away. Boda had been such a good friend to him down the years, while he'd been cowardly in the way he dealt with the truth about Hawkeye's demise. The blame could easily be shifted to T-Bone, but that wasn't totally fair. He could've – should've – told Boda a long time ago.

"Don't forget this," Boda handed over the Polaroid as the big man stepped out of the van, his leg still wrecked, but his heart full of hope. They both smirked at the sight captured in the image.

"Good luck," grinned Boda, before gliding away and leaving Tubbs alone on the pavement, his heart fluttering as the butterflies in his stomach suddenly broke free of their cocoons.

Tubbs limped towards home, although he really felt like skipping. Not that he was expecting anything to happen that night; he was too much of a pessimist for that. He was excited, that's all. He'd never felt anything like this. Ever. And he couldn't wait to get to know Petra, properly. He realised that she was much younger than him – a decade at least – but there was no denying the connection between them. However, when he opened the gate his house lay in total darkness and all his hopes faded at once.

He half-expected, half-hoped to see a note pinned to the front door, but she hadn't even had the courtesy to do that. She'd left him with nothing. He unlocked the door and stepped into the dark and silent interior. A couple of the cats circled his feet and demanded their supper in the usual manner, so Tubbs turned on the lights in the hope of seeing Victor among them. But he was nowhere to be seen, which was a bad sign, considering he'd been following Petra around all day.

He slowly made his way to the kitchen and opened two tins of tuna, and while he scraped the fish into the cats' bowls, he suddenly heard a voice, a siren singing and calling to him from somewhere, which in turn made his heart race once more.

Tubbs left the felines to it and followed the sound towards

the source. He leaned on the wall outside the closed door of the bathroom and listened to her sing. She had the voice of an angel, or at least a country singer.

After listening for a little while, he knocked the door and waited for an answer. The singing stopped at once.

"Al?" Petra called. "Come on in, I'm sorta decent!"

"Sort of?" Tubbs inquired without opening the door, just in case.

"Yeah. Don't be shy like, I'm covered in bubbles. Come on, I wanna see you."

Tubbs opened the door and stepped into the bathroom without looking at Petra. However, from the corner of his eye, he could see that she was telling the truth – the bath *was* filled with bubbles, and only Petra's head could be seen floating above the soapy fizz.

Petra watched him enter and became instantly worried because of the serious look that was splashed across his face.

"What happened? What d'you do?" she asked, as Tubbs turned to face her at last, while stroking the sleeping Victor, who was curled on top of a pile of towels next to the airing cupboard.

Tubbs slowly eased himself onto the closed toilet seat, gritting his teeth in response to the pain that ripped once more along his wounded leg.

"Al. Fuckin' hell, c'mon! What happened?"

Tubbs looked at her – his face ashen, his eyes glazed.

"Don't ask," he said sombrely, shaking his hanging head. "Things got a bit messy, but we got away just in time…"

"Shittin' hell!" Petra exclaimed. "You didn't… you know… fuck… just in time for *what*?"

"Look," Tubbs lifted the Polaroid so that Petra could see what they'd done to her captor. She sat up at once, exposing her perfect pair to her slightly stunned suitor, wiping her hands on a nearby towel and grabbing the photo for closer inspection. She looked at the image and Tubbs watched as her smile grew ever wider.

"Is that what I think it is?!" She shrieked, her accent echoing off the tiles. Tubbs nodded and Petra screamed with delight.

THE LAST HIT

"M R PARENTI! Wake up, Mr Parenti! We're preparing to land…" The heavily made-up, bottle-blonde, middle-aged stewardess gently shook Luca's shoulder, reeling him back to a state of semi-consciousness. She'd been servicing BA's first class passengers for some six years now, and was very experienced when it came to looking after the needs of rock stars, actors, models, sportsmen and other members of the so-called elite. By now she could recognise the signs and instantly knew that Signor Parenti was floating happily on an ocean of Valiums and G&Ts – a common cocktail among first class travellers of a certain ilk.

Luca slowly opened his eyes, thanked her and stretched his arms above his head. After watching him struggle with his safety belt, she helped him buckle up, before moving on. Luca closed his eyes once again as the pilot's voice told everyone on board that he was preparing to land at Heathrow airport.

Luca couldn't wait to get home. He missed the place itself, as well as his friends, both human and equine, every time he went away. And although he didn't relish the four-hour car journey back to Disgraceland, he was already looking forward to a nice Jacuzzi and a few cold beers with the boys before hitting the hay. After all, he had to do *something* to ease the stiffness induced by 36 hours in the company of two of Italy's most fit, eager and imaginative twins.

Apart from the time he spent with Caterina and Carolina, the tour had been a bit of a disaster. Things got off to a good start with three sold-out gigs, culminating with some serious fun with the twins back at the hotel after the Perugia show. However, the next day brought bad news – the Schillaci Theatre in Rome, where he was to play his last, and biggest, shows, had burnt down overnight, so the tour came to a premature end. Of course, this wasn't bad news for everyone – mainly Luca and his libido – as one night with the twins turned into two.

Darren, Sarge and Blim left him to it and headed to Milan to watch a match at the San Siro, leaving Luca to travel home alone, with nothing but a bad back, a sore cock and some great memories keeping him company. But at least he wouldn't have to drive home – the record company was sending a car; with the driver instructed to pick up a six pack of ice cold Tigers on the way.

"Don't go!" Petra pleaded, with tears in her eyes, as her man aimed for the front door and the darkness that lay beyond.

After almost a week in his company, she knew everything about him. Her initial instinct had been confirmed – he had indeed lived a life full of heartbreak and hardship in the shadow of death. But instead of being repulsed by his story and his calling, Petra was drawn nearer to this dark angel with every story he told her. After all, she too had played a major part in her parents' death. Not purposefully, of course, but she could empathise with Al's plight, especially on hearing how he was conned into the life by his mentor following his mother's untimely death. In fact, a week wasn't close to being enough time in his company; she wanted to love him for ever more. She'd lost so much already during her short life, and seeing Al fully pumped and heading west for a showdown with his mentor-turned-adversary was enough to make her heart implode inside her chest.

Like an echo of the happy couple that lived in the cabin all those years ago, Al and Petra spent most of their time in the garden, where they talked endlessly, shared stories and allowed their lives to quickly become entwined. However, their dream-like daytime relationship was almost overshadowed by the complexity of their bedroom-based bonding.

"What's wrong?" cooed Petra, as Al turned his back on her in bed for the second night in succession.

"Nothing. Just tired," came his curt reply. Tubbs hadn't shared a bed with anyone, except his cats, for many years and his monk-like existence had robbed him of any confidence he might have once possessed; not to mention any self-control.

Unlike every other man she'd ever been with, Al hadn't tried to fuck her once during the two nights they'd spent sleeping together in the same bed. They kissed and cuddled, fondled and fingered, licked and lapped at each other; but whatever they did, it always ended the same way; with Tubbs turning his back abruptly, leaving Petra confused, cold and unfulfilled.

Both nights, after turning his back on his lover-in-waiting, Tubbs lay there in the knowledge that this could not continue if their relationship was to develop into a serious one, as he hoped it would. On the second night, after listening to Petra's breathing grow deeper and quieter with every passing minute until, eventually, he was certain she was asleep, Tubbs slipped out of bed and made his way quietly to the bathroom, where he took off his spunk-soaked boxer-shorts and rinsed them under the tap before chucking them in the laundry basket, where last night's jizz-rag was waiting for them.

Petra felt the bed breathe a sigh of relief as Al got up and made his way to the bathroom. She could hear him pottering in there and knew at once what was going on. She'd had the same effect on plenty of others before him.

Wearing clean pants, Tubbs slipped quietly back under the covers, which made Petra turn to face him. She seemed to be smiling in her subconscious, and he hoped that her dreams were far better than this reality.

The same thing happened on the third night, namely heavy

petting followed by an unsubtle manoeuvre which left Petra staring at the cliff-face of Al's back. But this time, she reacted.

"No way, Al!" she exclaimed, grabbing his shoulder and yanking him onto his back. "Not again." This could not go on any longer, and anyway, she was sopping wet and choking for some action. She stared into his deer-in-the-headlight-eyes, reached down and felt the gooeyness that was gluing his boxers to his belly. But before she could do anything to resolve the situation, Al burst from the bed, grabbed his dressing gown and left.

She heard the patio door slide open, and lay back in the hope that he wouldn't drive off in his car. But when, after a minute, no engine had been heard, she got out of bed, grabbed one of Al's huge T-shirts from the drawer and made her way out into the night, on the trail of this wounded soldier.

In the light of the moon, she made her way down to the bottom of the garden; her whole body covered in goosebumps, her nipples poking through the cotton tee like a photo finish in a Zeppelin race. She found her man sitting with his back against his mother's palm tree, knees pulled up, head pushed down; Victor purring maniacally while prodding his brow against a protruding elbow. He heard her approach and lifted his gaze to reveal tears glistening on his cheeks. Without a word, Petra slipped in and straddled him, opening his robe, holding him tight. She wiped his tears, kissed his cheeks. She bit his lip, almost drawing blood. She whispered "I love you" in his ear, and felt his primeval response.

The following day, with the sex out of the way and comfortably behind them, they continued in much the same fashion, but with additional rutting, of course. And as they grafted in the garden and pottered around the house, they revealed their deepest darkest secrets and wildest dreams to one another. Petra reminisced about growing up in Merthyr – the good and the bad – her parents' passing and her dreams of becoming a professional singer-stroke-actress-stroke-dancer stroke-something. She was totally honest about her time selling tricks to the dregs and desperados of the Gurnos. She felt a bit weird revealing all, but she didn't want to keep anything from him. Not while he was being so frank about his life. What they both needed was a clean slate, and she soon found out that Al's needed even more Fairy Liquid than her own. A lot more, in fact.

Al started at the beginning; his earliest memories including his mother's vocation and his father's death; before moving on to their life with T-Bone, Foxy's murder and his consequent life as a hired gun and ganja wholesaler. She listened intently to the seemingly tall tales, but she knew they were true. She wasn't sure how to react to begin with, but on remembering how he didn't judge her when she told him her own story, she realised that what he needed was support, as he obviously wanted to turn his back on that part of his life.

"You know what makes me hate him most?" Al asked one lunchtime, as the lovers took a break from the floriculture and the fornicating.

"The lies? The deceit?"

"Aye. Of course. But more than that even…"

"What?"

"Well… it's the fact that he set me up from the very start. I mean, the way he… tricked me… I don't even know if that's the right word… anyway… *fuck*!"

Petra stroked his shoulder, chewed some bread and cheese while waiting for Al to regain his composure. T-Bone - this man, this monster – had ruined his so-called 'son'. Of that she was totally certain. Not only had he killed his mother, but he'd turned Al into something that he so clearly wasn't.

"D'you know that I can remember his exact words the day he recruited me. He said, 'You need a weapon for two reasons, Al. One, you'll need a gun if you're going to work for me. And two, you need a gun so you can hunt your mother's killer…' Can you believe that? He looked me in the eyes as he was saying it too. No remorse. No repentance. No shame. And this was only a few weeks, maybe a month after he'd killed her!"

Al laughed at this. Petra smiled, although she wasn't sure why.

"He's used me ever since, hasn't he? He's dangled this carrot before my nose in the knowledge that I'll *never* find out who killed my mother…"

"Until now."

"Aye."

Petra could sense that the guilt weighed heavily on Al's broad shoulders. Guilt for all he had done on T-Bone's behalf as a hitman and for being so easily suckered and allowing the old man to use him and get away with Foxy's murder all these years. Not to mention the guilt he felt for the secret he'd kept from his best friend for so long. And although Al hoped that by avenging his mother's murder, everything would somehow be ok, Petra wasn't so sure.

"I've *got* to go, Petra, or I'll never be free to…" Tubbs paused by the front door and looked into her eyes, searching for the right words to finish the sentence. But he saw his mother staring back and somehow couldn't find them.

"To *what*, Al?" Petra asked, sensing that she was close to hearing something important.

"To be *normal*," answered Tubbs, surprising himself by being so certain, so unafraid. He longed for a simple life, without complications: the complete opposite to his existence so far. His life had been one long series of obstacles and dramas, but now that he'd finally found peace and happiness with Petra, he yearned for something else.

Two days previously, Tubbs had done the rounds and delivered what he picked up from Disgraceland to his customers in the Cardiff area. He explained to each one that this could be the last time he'd see them. And although there were plenty of protestations, he was determined to loosen the shackles and live a simple life: just him and Petra, the garden and the cats. And it wasn't as if he needed the money – he was a very wealthy man, thanks to the cash he'd accumulated during his time working for T-Bone and selling Disgraceland's wares.

Boda had visited the cabin almost every day during the week, and the dragon that climbed Tubbs's right leg was now complete. A bit bloody and very sore, but finished at long last. Although Tubbs was eager to tell his friend the truth about his father's death, somehow the right moment never arose. Petra was convinced that Al was waiting for a moment that would never materialise, but also sympathised with his plight and the seriousness of what he had to tell him.

Tubbs hadn't been anywhere near Rudry either, although T-Bone had been a constant presence in his mind. And as their relationship neared its boiling point, Petra sensed a change in him, especially today as the showdown tick-tocked ever near.

"Look, Petra," Tubbs began, as his lover reached for her fags. Her hands shook as she lit one, but the smoke calmed her in an instant. He stepped to her and gently touched her face with one of his huge paws. Her scar was healing nicely, and then Vexl's mug flashed before his eyes. *How did he like his scars?* he wondered. "Look, Petra," he repeated. "I *have* to go. I *have* to do this. This is my last chance to be free. My *only* chance to be free in fact, and *our* only chance to have a future together. A *real* future. You know, like normal people. And that's something I'm not prepared to compromise on…"

Petra stared into his eyes; so gentle on the one hand, but beyond darkness on the other. "Just make sure you're back before breakfast, ok," she said with a smile, then kissed him hard and watched him go.

On the other side of the capital at roughly the same time, T-Bone struggled to open the armoury hidden beneath his office's wooden floor. His hips were so stiff that getting his hands on a piece of steel was almost impossible. However, after lying down and wriggling around for a little while, he managed to extract three weapons from his small arsenal, before using his desk to haul himself back to a standing position. He was definitely too old for this shit, he concluded correctly, but there was no turning back now. He checked the guns to ensure that they were loaded, before his eyes wondered and came to a halt on an image hanging on the wall. He stared at it for a while as the memories came flooding back. It was taken around 1984 at the Bandidos' annual barbecue. T-Bone smiled in the centre of the picture with one arm around Foxy on his right and the other around a be-vested young Al. He tried to remember if they were in fact *as* happy at the time as the photo suggested, but the sad truth was that he couldn't be sure. He looked from Foxy to her son, thanking the gods that the giant of a man he'd grown into had never discovered the truth about what happened to his mother. And after tonight, he'd never be able to either…

He placed one gun in his waistband, another in the holster he already wore under his jacket and the third, the smallest, in his pocket, and then limped out of the crumbling manor house.

Boda waved as the Polo passed him on the street outside Tubbs's cabin, but his friend didn't acknowledge him. Boda didn't think anything of it – he knew that Tubbs could be a right blind bastard sometimes; so on he went and parked the van on the drive.

He wasn't expected here today either, but he'd forgotten some needles the previous day, and was just popping in to collect them en route to another appointment. He crossed the gravel driveway and knocked on the door. No answer. Petra was probably in the shower or out in the garden or something, so he turned the handle and entered, at once hearing the soft sobbing nearby. He followed the blubbing and found Petra, head in her hands, sitting by the kitchen table.

"What's the matter? What happened?" Boda asked, genuinely concerned.

"Al…" came the answer, which didn't help at all.

"What *about* him? What's he done?"

"Nothen," came the confusing answer. Followed by "yet", which helped a little, but not a lot.

"What does *that* mean?"

"He's gone to meet T-Bone…" Petra looked up now, reaching for her half smoked ciggy.

"*And*? Come on, Petra, what's going on?"

"You've gorra go afta him, Bo'…"

"Why? He goes to see T-Bone all the time," Boda answered, properly perplexed.

"This time's a bit different… please Bo'… you've *gorra* help him…"

"Ok, ok. So where's he gone, and why's it different this time?"

"I can't tell you. He'll 'ave to explain himself."

"Fuckin' hell, Petra, this isn't the time to be cryptic!"

"I'm so scared, Bo'."

"Just tell me where he's gone. Rudry, is it?"

"No. Down west. Luca's place."

"Disgraceland?"

"Yeah, that's it. Disgraceland." And off he went, without his needles, leaving Petra where he found her, sobbing and smoking by the kitchen table.

Blod sat behind the wheel of his car in the far corner of the empty Brynhoffnant Arms car park. The pub had recently shut for refurbishment, which made it the perfect place for a rendezvous such as this. He watched the traffic flash by on the A487 on the other side of the hedgerow; the vehicles' lights strobing in the deepening darkness. He wondered how many lives had been lost on this particular road during his time living nearby. *Too many,* was his sad conclusion. The A487 between Cardigan and Aberystwyth was notorious for the number of accidents that happened on it each year. In fact, it seemed to him that the Grim Reaper himself probably had a holiday home in the area – a nice static caravan at Treddafydd perhaps – as not a week went by without a new name being added to the ever-increasing list of the deceased.

Blod pondered the possibility of T-Bone turning up without a gun. He laughed at the thought. *As if!* There was no chance of that happening, which is why he had a fully-loaded Browning 9mm semi-automatic pistol lying beside him on the passenger seat and a couple of shotguns in the boot, all borrowed from Luca's until now unnecessary private collection.

He wasn't sure how he'd react upon seeing Foxy's killer, but he didn't have long to wait until he found out…

Tubbs turned the Polo off the A487 before driving slowly down the dark and narrow country lane towards Disgraceland. He'd clocked Boda's van following him just this side of Llandysul, so when he stopped outside the gates, instead of inputting the code and going on in, he got out of the car and waited for his friend to catch up, before waving him over when the idiot stopped some hundred yards up the road, on a blind bend. Boda pulled up behind him, and got out himself.

"What're you doin', Bo'? Why d'you follow me?"

"I'm not too sure, dude. I saw you leave your gaff, looking angry. Well fucked off like. Petra was crying when I called in, blubbing something about T-Bone, and as you know I'm a sucker for damsels in distress. Anyway, here I am. But more to the point, what the fuck are *you* doing here?"

"You're about to find out. C'mon."

Blod watched the car pull in. He knew it was T-Bone even before the bastard killed his engine and stepped out into the night to stretch his legs and have a look around. Even in the dark, Blod could see that the once fearsome killer was now no more than an old man with bad hips and a slightly humped back. Amazingly, he felt a little sorry for him, before remembering what he'd done to the love of his life.

He started the engine and flooded the car park with his full-beams. T-Bone turned as the gardener inched slowly towards him. He opened the window as he approached and grabbed the gun off the seat. The hatred simmered as he came face to face with the man who'd ruined his life and robbed him of any happiness. If it wasn't for Al's part in the plan, he'd have either shot T-Bone in the face, run him over or beaten him to death with his bare hands without giving the cunt a chance to say a word.

Blod levelled the gun at T-Bone and brought the car to a stop. He switched off the lights, put it in neutral and stepped out, the gun pointed at the old man the whole time.

The bandit smiled, which made Blod angry. "Turn around and put your hands on the roof of the car."

"What are you, fucking CID?"

Blod ignored the jibe and patted him down. As expected, T-Bone was armed. Well-armed as well. He had a Magnum .357 in a shoulder holster, a Baretta 92 tucked into his waistband and a hunting knife in his boot.

"I said *unarmed*," Blod spat, tossing the weapons onto the front passenger seat of his own car.

"Touché," replied T-Bone, with another smile tickling his tache.

"If you move, I'll shoot you," Blod promised, before flicking on a flash-lamp and proceeding to give the old man's car a quick once-over, in case the sly bastard had any other weapons concealed somewhere. Keeping one eye on the biker, Blod searched under the seats, the glove-box and anywhere else that came to mind, but didn't find a thing.

"Follow me," he spat, before getting back behind the wheel and waiting for T-Bone to get in his car and make a three-point turn.

After turning the car, T-Bone slowly followed the gardener across the car park towards the exit, all the while prising open the plastic compartment between the steering wheel and the dashboard using his house key, where he'd concealed a DB380 pistol before leaving Rudry. The tiny handgun – a girl's gun, without a doubt – might not have packed as much of a punch as the ones the gardener had already taken from him, but it was far better than stepping unarmed into the unknown. He placed it in his jacket pocket, and turned onto the road towards Tresaith.

With the key Blod had left under the plant pot, Tubbs opened the back door to Disgraceland and stepped into the kitchen. As promised, the place was empty and the alarm hadn't been activated.

"Where is everyone?" asked Boda, relieved that it didn't appear that he'd have to face Pennar again tonight.

"Out," answered Tubbs. The adrenalin started rushing and his best friend's presence did not help matters at all.

"So *why* exactly are we here? What're we up to?"

"Follow me." Tubbs ignored the questions and led the way down the hall and through the luxurious lounge at the front of the house to the small adjoining office, located at its far end.

On reaching the study, Boda switched on the light and sat in the leather swivel-chair behind the desk.

"Fuck sake, Bo'!" Tubbs cursed and turned it off again, before closing the connecting door carefully behind him, but leaving it slightly ajar so that he could eavesdrop on the conversation that would soon be taking place.

"What the fuck's going on, Tubbs? Serious now, what *are* you doing?"

"Shhhut up, Bo'!" Tubbs almost exploded, which had the desired effect. Boda joined him at the door in time to hear footsteps approaching. While standing there listening, still none the wiser as to what they were doing and why, Boda noticed that his friend held a gun in his hand and it dawned on him that this visit to Disgraceland was slightly more serious than the last.

"Drink?" asked Blod, gesturing for T-Bone to sit down in one of the leather chairs over by the unlit fireplace.

"Whisky. No ice," came the curt answer. T-Bone looked around as he took his seat, marvelling at the magnificence of what he assumed was the gardener's mansion. He wasn't expecting this at all. Old Blod had done well for himself, that was for sure.

Blod filled two crystal glasses with one of Luca's favourite malts. He passed one to the Bandit before sitting down opposite him and taking a sip of his own. While the whisky warmed his throat, Blod wondered what the best way of extracting the truth from T-Bone would be, but before saying anything, the old biker started yapping, making life very easy for the gardener.

"I thought it was money you were after, but I'm not so sure now that I've seen your house…" T-Bone used his empty hand to signal their surroundings.

"*Money!*" Blod saw his chance and laughed aloud at T-Bone's presumption, without revealing the truth about Disgraceland's tenure. "And how much do you think Foxy's life is worth exactly?"

T-Bone ignored the question; after all, he didn't have the answer. "What *do* you want then?"

"An explanation."

"An *explanation*?"

"Yes. But I don't want to know *why* you killed Foxy, because there isn't a reason in this world that could justify your action. What I want to know is how you can live with yourself? How do you sleep at night, knowing what you did?"

"With some difficulty and plenty of bourbon," came the flippant answer, which would go some way to confirming the truth to Al, Blod hoped. The murderer supped greedily from the crystal glass, hoping that the whisky would calm his nerves, because contrary to the cool impression he was trying to exude, he was certain there was more going on here than he was aware of. He placed his right hand in his jacket pocket and felt the cold steel within; so glad that he'd outsmarted the gardener, again.

"What about Al?" asked Blod. The question grabbed T-Bone's attention, his cockiness disappearing at once on hearing his son's name. But before he could answer or respond, the door to the lounge burst open, and in stepped Luca; larger than life, smiling like a lottery winner, and still flying off all the Vals and gin and lager flowing through his body.

"Yes, boys! I'm baaaaaaaaaaaaaaaaaaaaaack!" he bellowed, before his life took an unexpected turn for the worse thanks to a single bullet from T-Bone's hidden handgun.

Luca fell to the floor holding his chest, plunging Blod and Tubbs's well-laid plan into unexpected chaos. The scarlet sprayed everywhere as the singer stared at the wound in disbelief. His mouth was agape, but no scream escaped. Just blood. Lots and lots of blood.

Blod joined him on the floor in an instant, top off and holding his cotton shirt over Luca's laceration in an attempt to stem the flow.

"Stay with me Luca!" he barked, before repeating the command over and over again. He grabbed his face and stared into his empty eyes. "Come on Luca, don't fuckin' die now!"

Blod turned to look at T-Bone, but the biker was already on his feet, standing within a few feet of the drama, holding a gun to the gardener's head. With ice cold calm and a cruel smile tickling the corners of his mouth, T-Bone relished reciting the last rites.

"I should have finished the job back at the Safari Inn. There's no escape this time…"

T-Bone cocked the gun.

Blod closed his eyes.

T-Bone felt the cold steel on the back of his neck. The world froze as he watched an anonymous hand carefully take the gun from his grasp. He turned slowly and came face to face with his every nightmare: he saw Foxy herself staring back at him through her only son's ardent eyes.

Blod opened his eyes and saw Al and Boda standing there, both holding a gun to T-Bone's head.

"How's Luca doing?" asked Tubbs.

"Not good. He's losing a lot of blood…" Blod answered.

"Hang in there Luca, we'll be with you in a minute."

He hasn't got a minute! screamed Blod's sub-conscious, but he didn't say a word, it was too late already, as Luca was fast losing his battle with death, right there on the floor of his favourite room.

"Do it, Tubbs!" Boda hissed. "You heard what he did! He killed your mam! He deserves to die."

Tubbs cursed himself. He should have done this a week ago? He knew the truth as soon as Blod told him and at least that way Luca wouldn't be lying in a pool of blood, on the brink of taking his last breath. Tubbs held the gun to his mentor's head but couldn't pull the trigger. T-Bone looked into his eyes and smiled. He knew at once that Al had lost his bottle. Tubbs stared back at his white hair, grey eyes and cold black heart. His head echoed with every lie that had ever flowed from T-Bone's mouth over the years. It hurt, no doubt, but Tubbs still couldn't end the saga.

"*Why*?" he asked, as T-Bone's eyes darted in every direction but couldn't meet his gaze.

"She *betrayed* me, Al. What was I *supposed* to do?"

Tubbs stepped to the desk, opened the top drawer and found what he was looking for at once.

"After everything I gave her… gave *you*… how did she repay me? By fucking the fucking gardener!" Tubbs stepped to him and covered his mouth with Sellotape then wrapped the tape twice around the back of his head.

"That should stop the lies for a little while," he said, before lifting his gun once again and looking into T-Bone's eyes. With his finger over the trigger, he willed himself to do what he came here to do. But he couldn't. He *just* couldn't. His hand started shaking; the sweat poured from his forehead, before the tears joined in and cascaded down his cheeks. Through the fog, he could see T-Bone smirking behind the makeshift muzzle as his eyes danced with danger. But he still couldn't kill him. Down came the gun, Tubbs defeated.

"Blod."

The gardener turned to look at Tubbs.

"What?"

"Would *you* like the pleasure?"

Blod shook his head. "I'm no killer, Al. Even if he does

deserve to die, I'm not the one to do it…" Then he turned back to Luca, and went looking for the poor soul's pulse in his wrist, under his chin, anywhere…

"Boda?" Tubbs turned to his best friend, who was still holding his gun to T-Bone's temple.

"*Me?*"

"Aye."

"Why would I want to do it, dude?"

"Because this is the man that killed your father…"

Boda stared at Tubbs – his eyes ablaze, the adrenalin rushing – then turned his attention to T-Bone in search of confirmation. The truth was there in the old man's eyes and the smirk behind the Sellotape. Boda remembered the last time he'd seen his old man, on the morning of his death. Hawk, as always, had a huge hangover. That was his default setting before noon. That said, he always had time for his only son. He'd promised to take Boda hunting for his eighteenth birthday, up in the hills on some estate that belonged to a dodgy acquaintance, no doubt. But, of course, they never went, and Boda had never held so much as a BB gun before this very moment. As a lifelong Bandido, he could talk the talk, of course; but now he was about to discover whether he could also walk the walk. He breathed deeply through the nose, composed himself, and pulled the trigger. As Boda's whole body recoiled in response to the handgun's awesome power, he watched as the Bandit's skull exploded all over the wall, furniture as well as his contorted face. T-Bone's body fell to the floor with a thud, then Boda turned the gun on Tubbs, who stood leaning on the desk, his back to the blood-soaked scene.

When Tubbs heard the blast from his friend's pistol, followed by the shower of crimson and the unmistakable thud of T-Bone's corpse hitting the floor, his very soul was torn in two by the opposing forces of relief and regret. He was free. At last. His mother's murderer was dead on the floor behind him. His contract fulfilled, the cuffs unlocked. If only he hadn't loved her killer with all his heart not so long ago. His thoughts turned to Foxy, then quickly to Petra. He had to get home to her. He needed to hold her. He needed to be held. He slowly turned to face reality, and came face to face with his best friend-turned-executioner.

Boda watched the tears stream down his oldest friend's cheeks, which caused the gun to start shaking in his grasp. His mind raced, befuddled by the unexpected revelation. How long had Tubbs known the truth?

"Why didn't you tell me, man?" He asked.

"I tried... b-b-b-but...?" Tubbs tried to answer, his eyes boring into his best friend's soul in search of some compassion.

"But *what?*"

Tubbs looked away, saw Luca lying lifeless in Blod's arms.

"But *what?*" Boda raised his voice this time; the wrath suddenly possessing him, the resentment exploding from deep within. His whole body shook with rage, the gun almost touching Tubbs's nose.

"I'm sorry, Bo'. I d-d-didn't know how. I j-j-just didn't know h-h-how..." Tubbs's voice trailed off as he watched his best friend closely; trigger finger poised regardless of his trembling body, the pain so apparent on his face. But his anger towards Tubbs subsided as Boda realised that he wasn't the only one to come face to face with the man who had murdered his parent tonight. And as his own tears began to flow, he lowered his gun and stepped towards his best friend, before embracing the big man and holding him tight.

ACKNOWLEDGEMENTS

Big thanks to the wife, the kids, the old man and my bro, mainly for putting up with me and my nonsense.

Thanks also to my editor, Eifion Jenkins
www.eifionjenkins.co.uk
for all his hard work and thoroughness;

and to Lefi, Eirian and the rest of the team at *Y Lolfa*, for their continued support.

Cover designed by Jamie Hamley
www.jamiehamley.com

I'd also like to acknowledge the financial support of the Welsh Books Council.

ABOUT THE AUTHOR

Llwyd Owen was born and raised in Cardiff, where he still lives to this day. When not writing fiction, he works as a translator.

He has published six Welsh language novels and won the Welsh Book of the Year prize in 2007. His first English novel, *Faith, Hope & Love* was published in 2010 and is available from **www.ylolfa.com**

For more information about the author, visit **www.llwydowen.co.uk**

The Last Hit is just one of a whole range of
publications from Y Lolfa. For a full list of
books currently in print, send now for your
free copy of our new full-colour catalogue.
Or simply surf into our website

www.ylolfa.com

for secure on-line ordering.

TALYBONT CEREDIGION CYMRU SY24 5HE
e-mail ylolfa@ylolfa.com
website www.ylolfa.com
phone (01970) 832 304
fax 832 782